NEAR DEATH
DEATH'S DOORSTEP SERIES

MIA HALL

DEDICATION

Thank you to the readers! You've made my dragon dreams a reality!

Sign up for Mia's Newsletter to find out about new releases.
Put the following in your browser window:
mailerlite.com/webforms/landing/e1d4k4

Covers by Ammonia Book Covers

The day was the fifteenth of December. Christmas break had just started. Kiera watched from her dorm room window as all the Dreadmore Academy students piled into their cars in the back parking lot and sped off to join their families for Christmas. Others lugged their suitcases or secretly used hovering magic to get to the front of the campus so they could get picked up. The air was bright and filled with excitement, despite the chill in the air. There was only a light layer of snow on the ground.

Kiera had just received a text from her father. He'd been on his way to get her when his car got a flat. It would take at least five hours to fix since he had a flat two months ago and hadn't replaced the backup tire he used back then. He had suggested she carpool with Ben, same as she had on the way to Dreadmore, but Kiera hadn't answered yet.

She had no energy today. She had woken up in the middle of the night, vaguely recalling a strange dream about someone being in her room, then vanishing. It was probably all in her head, but it still nagged at her.

To make matters worse, there was some part of her soul or magic or both tugging her toward the middle of campus. The feeling discouraged her from leaving, giving her a sense of dread when she thought about spending Christmas with her family and away from the pulling sensation. She wasn't sure where this feeling originated from and why her magic was so insistent on keeping her here, but it was affecting her mood.

Kiera texted her father back after some deliberation.

Is it okay if i stay on campus?

Her fingers were cold. The heating in this building wasn't that good. She'd need to light a magic fire or something to warm herself up.

There was a pause, then her father replied.

Best ask your mother about it. What's the problem? I thought you were all packed and ready to go.

I am. It's just—

Kiera stopped and backspaced, erasing the words.

I'm sick and don't want to vomit in the car. Plus, Mom was set to work overtime anyway so i won't see much of her over the holidays.

Another pause. Her father was likely analyzing her words, trying to make sure nothing was wrong. He was the paranoid type, just like she used to be, and he'd become even more nervous when things started going wrong in the magical academy.

Her time at Dreadmore had always been fraught with conflict. First, she and her best friend Ben had an encounter with a girl who was paralyzing play-boys on campus. She had planned to eventually kill them. It was pure coincidence that Kiera stumbled onto the killer on the school path and stopped her in the nick of time.

Then, during the next semester, Kiera acciden-tally opened an evil fairy door all by herself. It had been unearthed during the school's yearly renova-tions and it was only thanks to the headmaster and her homeroom teacher that the fairies were sent back to their lair.

Finally, just last semester, some gargoyles had attacked her. That same headmaster and teacher had protected her, but she was still worried one might emerge again and finish the job the others failed at. Plus, there was the ominous figure in her room that might be real or fake, as well as this nagging feeling telling her to head downstairs and approach the middle of the campus for some unknown reason.

It was a lot to take in. It was a miracle she wasn't a shaking ball of paranoia right now.

Plus, well, there was one more thing bugging her. As soon as she woke up this morning, she'd become overwhelmed by a sense of loss. It was like someone she knew had died, but she couldn't remember who.

I'm not in any danger, Kiera added to reassure her dad, though that might not be entirely true.

If whatever was happening to her was real and not in her head, someone or something was messing with her. The only problem was, she had no idea who or why.

Well, tell your mother, her father texted back. *And maybe ask if Ben wants to stay with you. I'd feel better letting you stay if he was there too.*

The teachers and staff are still here, Kiera replied. *But i will. Thanks, Dad.*

She texted Ben next, who replied by saying he'd only stay if Meiying and the others chose to remain too. That prompted her to text Tucker, Sally, and Meiying. Sally refused to stay, since she had a family reunion to get to, and Meiying said the same. Tucker was the only one who agreed to wait with them.

I feel like there's something I'm missing, Tucker admitted through text. But i don't know what it is. I'm hoping to figure it out by the end of the holidays.

That was weird. It was almost the same as Kiera's situation.

Tucker agreed to stay, she texted Ben after Tucker confirmed. *But Meiying has to visit family. Her grandparents flew in for Christmas.*

Ben sent a sad face emoji, then a grimacing one. *Fine. If your dad wants me to stay, i will. Plus—*

There was a pause as he continued typing for a while, implying he was typing things out, then erasing them over and over again. He must be worrying about their strange experiences as much as Kiera was. Finally, he finished. *I feel like something's wrong in my head, so I'm not too keen on leaving either. Lunch at noon?* That was just like him, cutting to the chase without a single transitional word.

Sure.

Then Kiera invited Tucker along. She needed to discuss these feelings with anyway. Plus, if Ben was experiencing it too, it was probably serious. The question was, had the entire school been affected by this weird phenomenon, or was it just the three of them? And what did they have that connected them but no one else? Tucker was just some guy who weaved into Kiera and Ben's friendship group easily, then he helped Sally and Meiying join too. They didn't have anything else in common.

Come to think of it, how did Kiera meet Tucker again? She couldn't recall their first meeting.

After telling her mom the plan, Kiera headed to the cafeteria, ignoring the pull toward the center of the campus. She'd follow that tug later. For now, she wanted to talk to Tucker and Ben so they could confirm she wasn't going crazy.

2

Kiera had never seen the cafeteria during a holiday before. Normally, it was filled to the brim with students, some visible and some not, and the air was always filled with the chatter of excited or exhausted students. The meals, a mixture of all cultures and tastes, were always overflowing on the buffet tables.

Now, there were maybe ten students at the most, seated sparsely among the tables. The long, plastic tables had been replaced, making room for more personal seating arrangements. The food was only manned by one chef and it didn't have as much diversity. Kiera had to settle for some chili heaped on top of a baked potato. The chef offered some magical dust that would amplify the flavor, but she wasn't in the mood for anymore magic today. There was enough of it whirling around inside her.

Tucker and Ben were already at a table in the corner so it was easy enough to find them. Ben had his back against the wall and he was eyeing everyone entering. Kiera had a guess at who he was watching for.

"Keeping an eye out for Professor Gillis?" she asked, referring to her homeroom teacher, Kent Gillis. They all knew he was a bit of creep and probably delved into dark magic. Kiera herself took some special classes he'd offered, but he would always erase hers and the other thirteen students' memories after class ended. It was apparently to prevent their minds from caving or becoming over-loaded. It was still eerie, though, and the boys agreed.

"Something about him's not right," Ben commented, sneering at the door. "I wouldn't be surprised if he wiped *my* memory of something. That would explain why I feel so weird right now."

"You two haven't even met," Kiera said, laughing.

"But I feel like I have." Ben shook his head, waving it away. His blond hair was swept under a black baseball cap today and since Meiying, his girl-friend, wasn't around to see him, he wore all sweats.

"It might just be because you talk about him so much. I don't know."

"No, let's not brush this off," Tucker intervened.

Unlike Ben, Tucker was dressed in nice clothes despite it being the holidays. He wore a posh pair of black jeans, coupled with a blue button-up that complimented his dark hair and skin. "I'm beginning to think all of us had our memories wiped, though I can't be sure why that is. If you feel like you met Professor Gillis but don't remember ever doing so, that might be where the memories lie."

"So you think he erased our memories?" Kiera was skeptical. She didn't like the teacher but couldn't think of a reason for him to do such a thing. "Why would he do that?"

"That's the thing." Tucker chuckled. "We can't remember why."

"So, it's a mystery." Ben brightened at the thought of solving a crime. "Maybe he did something horrible and we caught him in the act!"

"Keep your voice down," Kiera hissed. "But... I agree."

So did Tucker. He pulled them all closer and they began discussing what it could be. They tried to correlate where their fuzzy memories lay, but it was hard to because you couldn't figure out what you couldn't remember until you had to remember it. So far, all they had was the memory of Ben meeting Professor Gillis. Well, that and meeting Tucker in the first place. When Kiera brought it up, Tucker immediately spoke as though it should be obvious.

"That's silly. We met in the library. You were... I was..." He frowned, stumped. "You're right. That memory's gone too. But that happened over a year ago, before Professor Gillis even came to the school. So he couldn't be the cause of the memory loss."

"Maybe he erased something that happened back then too. Like maybe... I don't know." Kiera kept feeling the answer right on the tip of her tongue before it evaded her. "This is giving me a headache."

"Same," Ben groaned, finishing the last of his food and shoving the empty plate away. "Can we take a break? I don't like feeling this way."

Kiera nodded but hesitated, wondering if she should tell them about the feeling pulling her toward the center of campus. Even though she was on the ground floor of the cafeteria, she could still feel it tugging downwards. At first, she assumed whatever it was had been pulling her downwards because her dorm room was on the top floor. Now she knew that wasn't the case. This tugging feeling wanted her to go underground, which was silly.

She decided she wouldn't tell them about this feeling. If it was telling her to dig underground, then it probably wasn't a real concern. It had to be the aftermath of that weird dream she'd already forgotten from last night.

"Let's take a walk around campus," Tucker suggested. "Maybe it'll trigger some of the memories, or the lack thereof. We could practice some magic too, since we have nothing but time right now."

"Sounds good," Ben said. "Kiera?"

Kiera agreed. If something evil was happening in Dreadmore, she wanted to nip it in the bud before it got worse. She'd had enough of getting attacked and nearly eaten by monsters. It was time to be proactive.

3

Taking a stroll through the grounds didn't dredge up any new memories—only old, traumatic ones. As Kiera walked past the auditorium where the Halloween party had occurred in October, she noted how the pillars at each corner of the building were empty. There used to be tall gargoyles up there. Then someone brought them to life and made them try to kill her. She'd had to fight them off alone until the headmaster arrived to save her.

There. There was a part of that memory she was missing. She couldn't recall the attacks clearly.

"What do you guys remember from the gargoyle attacks?" she asked. Sadly, neither Tucker nor Ben had seen much of the beasts. They'd been inside the auditorium when it happened and neither of them had their memories of the event tampered with.

Dissatisfied, Kiera felt herself shutting down. She needed a nap. "I'm ready to head home. This is pointless."

"Don't talk like that," Tucker said, always the encouraging one. "We'll figure this out eventually. Besides, we have two to three weeks to investigate. There's no need to rush."

"I have some game sales I need to check online anyway," Ben said, acting positive for once. He'd softened up after he got a girlfriend. "I'll go back to the dorm with you."

Tucker sighed. "I guess I'll go too. I hate to admit but this *does* feel like a dead end."

So they all headed back together. There was a dorm building specifically for second-years like them. Ben lived on the first floor, Tucker on the second, and Kiera on the top floor where the walls had extra insulation for complete silence.

The hallways were eerily empty and a little darker than normal. The silence made Kiera jump when the elevator they were waiting for dinged.

"Ladies first," Ben said as the elevator door opened. He gestured toward Tucker, who laughed.

Kiera rolled her eyes. "Sarcasm doesn't work on Tucker," she told Ben as she stopped into the elevator first. "It works better on—" Wait, who did it work better on again?

All three of them frowned in confusion as they stepped on. They all felt the absence.

Then, they started pressing the buttons for their floors. Kiera pressed T for top. Ben didn't press anything, and Tucker pressed four.

"Four?" Ben frowned at the buttons as the door closed on them. "I thought you lived on the second floor."

"I do. Huh?" Tucker stared at the elevator, as though *it* had been the one to press the wrong button. "That's weird."

"Is there someone on the fourth floor you're planning to meet?" Ben asked, nudging Tucker in a suggestive way.

"No. Not a girl, anyway. Hmm." Tucker looked genuinely stumped, which made Kiera's heart leap.

"Wait! Maybe what we need to find it on the fourth floor!" she shouted. "It could be connected to our lost memories!"

"Oh!" Tucker grinned. "Good point."

"So let's get off there," Ben said, "And Tucker can follow his instincts to the right room."

"But now that I'm *thinking* about it, I doubt I can find it," Tucker countered. "It has to be done subconsciously. I think my body remembers but my mind doesn't."

"We can at least give it a shot." Kiera didn't feel like giving up after all. This faint bit of hope had revived her energy. She could have a nap later.

Tucker shrugged. "Okay. Let's go." He shut his eyes, as though trying to let his body guide him blind. "By the way, do either of you know any spells for recalling forgotten things?"

"I could do some research in the library tonight," Kiera admitted. "But if this is a powerful spell, I doubt we'd have the skills to take it off ourselves. Plus, if it truly is the professor doing it, he probably prepared for that and created counter measures."

"Scary," Ben muttered. "Even though I haven't met him, he scares the crap out of me."

Kiera felt the same way. How on Earth had she managed to attend not only homeroom but also extra classes with him without getting creeped out?

They stayed silent as Ben led them down the hall. He would occasionally stop in front of a door, then shake his head, walk back to the elevator, and start again. He continued trying to retrace steps he couldn't remember, but every time, he insisted something was wrong.

"I feel like it's around here," he said, pointing at

three doors leading into individual dorms. "But I can't be sure which one."

"Should we knock?" Kiera asked, stumped. They couldn't ask staff for help since all they had to use as an excuse to open the door was "we have a feeling we've been in this room before."

"All the students have left for the holidays," Tucker pointed out, looking equally unsure how to proceed.

Kiera was trying to think up some other solution when Ben started trying the doorknobs, twisting them to see if any had been accidentally left unlocked.

"Ben!" Kiera hissed. "I'm pretty sure that's illegal."

"It's this or using magic to see through the walls. At least this way, we won't have unlawful magic use charges alongside breaking and entering, right?" Ben asked, then grinned when one of them opened. "Got one."

Kiera held her breath as Ben swung open the door. For some reason, she was expecting a monster to leap out. Her vague, not-memories made her think of dark shadows and monster silhouettes when she tried to recall them. She wouldn't be surprised if the things they'd forgotten were amnesia-causing beasts.

Instead of being leaped upon, all they saw inside was a small, cluttered room. The desk against the wall was piled high with books on both necromancy and general magic. The closet was filled with boys' clothes, including a few expensive suits, and the bed was perfectly made with silk sheets.

"A boy's room," Tucker commented, studying all the personal objects Kiera was looking at. "Wealthy, by the looks of it."

"Do you see any names?" Kiera asked as Ben pulled a box out from under the bed. Both he and Kiera bent down to see what was inside, but the contents surprised her. There was a high school yearbook from tenth grade. It belonged to a prestigious and expensive institution in the neighboring state. Next to it were some family pictures of a young, brown-haired boy Kiera didn't recognize, standing with his parents. Something about his handsome face nagged her, but she couldn't recall his name or if she'd ever met him. Maybe she'd passed him in the hall a few times.

Kiera started sorting through the pictures, then paused when Ben held one up.

"Isn't this the headmaster?" he asked, pointing at a photo of the same teenage boy standing next to the headmaster. They looked related, sharing the same facial structure and hair color, though they weren't identical.

Tucker nodded. "Maybe it's his son?" He was frowning now, probably experiencing the same déjà vu Kiera was. "No, that doesn't seem right."

Ben studied the photo suspiciously, then started digging through the box again. Kiera was trying to remember ever meeting this boy when Ben spoke her name.

"Kiera," he said, then held up a new picture, dumbfounded. Kiera felt the same when she laid eyes on it.

It was a picture of that boy yet again, or rather a picture he took himself, and Kiera was next to him, smiling shyly at the camera. They were standing really close to each other, so close that—

Her heart began to pulse and she knew this wasn't just some stranger she had passed in the halls or shared a class with. They were close and, if this feeling in her chest was real, they had dated.

This boy, whoever he was, must have been her boyfriend, but she couldn't recall him at all.

"What is going on?" she whispered, her heart pounding frantically.

"I think it's obvious," Tucker said somberly after taking the photo from Ben and studying it. "Someone has erased our memory of this boy. Now

—now that I'm looking at this, I think I've known him a long time. There are so many blanks in my memory and when I look at his picture, I feel something... weird."

Kiera felt the same way. Who was this boy? And who had erased their memories of him?

Ben was the one to finally put the pieces together. "If this boy is related to the headmaster, that means he's related to the professor too. I bet Kent doesn't want us talking to this kid for some reason. Maybe it's his brother or nephew." Ben was using the professor's first name now, so maybe he used to say it that way before the memory loss happened.

Ben's explanation made sense to Kiera, especially since it explained why she disliked Professor Gillis—or rather, Kent—so much.

"We need to report this to the headmaster," Tucker said and Kiera nodded immediately.

"Let's take the box with us," she added, taking the photo of her and the boy from Tucker and hiding it in her pocket. The sense of attachment was strong, even though she still couldn't technically remember the guy. Letting someone else hold that picture felt wrong.

"Wonder where he is?" Ben commented as they prepared to leave. He took one last look around the room, at the clothes and suitcase still resting in the closet. "Doesn't look like he packed up anything for the break."

"If he's wealthy, he might not need to," Tucker replied thoughtfully, but even he seemed unsure. "Let's just hope this is a simple misunderstanding, rather than something serious like last year."

"Right." Ben led the way out of the room. "Anything but killer fairies. I can't deal with those things again."

"Don't remind me," Kiera grumbled as they headed out. She was determined to solve this mystery before any of them got hurt.

❧ 4 ☙

The cold breeze blew dead leaves past their feet as they marched along the concrete path toward the staff building. It was located at the very front of the campus and looked more like a castle than a school office. Kiera almost wished they had upgraded *everything* to make it look modern. There was something eerie about magic being mixed with old buildings, especially when buildings these old belonged in Europe, not America. It made her wonder whether they'd just designed the buildings to *look* old, magically shipped them here from overseas, or if they actually were as old as they looked.

That would imply ancient, mythical creatures could be right under their feet or behind them in the woods. An old fairy prison had been hidden in the library walls, after all. Maybe there was more that hadn't been discovered yet, even by the older staff.

"What's the plan?" Ben whispered as they approached the staff building. It loomed over them, the many dark windows resembling eyes watching their every move. That must be why Ben was whispering, as though someone could hear them despite this entire area being nearly empty for the holidays.

"Sneak in and tell the headmaster what we found," Tucker said quickly. He was the one carrying the box. "I'll cast a seeing spell to check for any spies. I suggest you give us a stealth spell too, Ben."

"Right." Ben paused to think up the right spell, cast it, then turned back to Tucker and Kiera. "What if the headmaster is in on this scheme? How do we know we can trust him?"

Kiera had considered that too. "Should we tell someone else? Or maybe several people at once?"

"Who else would we tell? Our parents? We don't exactly have solid proof to warrant a drive all the way here," Tucker countered. "All we know is we forgot someone and he has a picture of himself with Kiera in his room. That's it. It's strange but I'm not sure if it's enough to call the police over."

Kiera nodded but still felt nervous. "Should we

split up before we go in?" They had reached the back door now and were all too scared to touch it.

"No way! Are you kidding?" Ben hissed. "That's how people wind up dead in horror movies. We're going together or not at all."

"I agree," Tucker said, though he didn't use the same tone as Ben. "I'll go first. Kiera, ready some attack spells in case we need to defend ourselves."

Kiera nodded, glad she could be of some use. Her necromancy made her both a useful healer and an attacker if necessary. While the other two could focus on stealth and mechanical magic, she could be the brawn to their brains. That wasn't a position she ever imagined being in when she first applied to this school. Back then, it wouldn't have suited her to take an active role.

Now, she was a new person, hardened by over a year of training, difficulties, and attacks. She also knew her worth. Not only was her talent on full display now, but Ben and her other friends—and maybe this nameless boy too—had shown her she was valued and loved.

Kiera hardened herself as they crept down the eerily silent halls of the building, heading for the stairs. An elevator might lead them right into the path of a culprit. It was better to take the stairs than risk getting caught.

They did pass a few teachers on their way through the floors, since some of the adults didn't leave for the Christmas break, but none of them batted an eye at the teenagers. Kiera kept an eye on the adults as they walked past, noting how casually some of them dressed now that most of the students were gone. It reminded Kiera that she shouldn't be here. She should be at home, enjoying her freedom from classes and studying. Instead, she was yet again facing an unknown enemy.

Tucker finally turned a corner and they were within sight of the headmaster's wooden door. His name, Philip Gillis, was on a golden plaque above the hardwood doorframe. It was the same last name Kiera saw in the boy's yearbook. They had to be related—the headmaster, Kent, and the mystery boy.

Tucker stopped them a few feet away from the door and pressed himself against the wall. A second later, Kiera understood why. There were two loud voices coming from the office and neither of them sounded happy.

"You really want to know why I'm asking?" the headmaster was shouting at someone. Kiera had never heard him shout before. It was a strange difference from him calm, friendly demeanor during announcements. "Because regardless of the blood we share, I still can't trust you after every-thing you've done, and I was having him watch over you to make sure you didn't fall back into your old habits."

"Who's he talking to?" Ben whispered. Kiera and Tucker shrugged. They got their answer a moment later.

"So you're telling me," Professor Gillis, Kent, replied a little more calmly. "You enlisted a child to spy on me. That's pathetic, Charles."

"I go by Phil now," the headmaster interrupted. "I stopped using that name after what you did in university. I want to separate myself from that boy who followed you so blindly." The two must be close, or at least used to be before whatever it was Kent did got between them. Kiera was brimming with curiosity about Kent's past now.

"Right, right." She could almost hear Kent shrug. "Always the goody two shoes."

"And Ezra is hardly a child anymore," the head-master added, ignoring his insult. "He's becoming everything you weren't. Responsible, trustworthy—"

"He got caught up in three different evil schemes in only three semesters. That worse than I was back then," Kent cut in. "You really think he didn't have anything to do with those events?

Maybe he was the one causing them. He was the one factor associated with all three incidents, after all."

"Or maybe that was *you* trying to make him look bad in front of his peers. He is your rival. You said so yourself when it was announced he'd be taking your role."

"I couldn't care less about that role."

Kiera couldn't get past the feeling that they were prying into private family business. She looked to Tucker, waiting for him to either knock on the door or walk away. This Ezra person might be the very person *they* were trying to remember. If the headmaster was on the mystery boy's side—it certainly sounded like he was—then going in to explain what they'd just found might be the piece of evidence the headmaster needed.

"They sound like they're working together," Ben whispered, his voice feeling like it was inside Kiera's head rather than in the air. He must be using a spell to keep their voices silent. "How do we know we can trust the headmaster?"

"I don't think they're working together," Tucker countered quickly. "But now I definitely think Kent is up to something."

They were all referring to him as Kent now. All

respect, or at least politeness, toward their superior was gone.

"Maybe we shouldn't use magic," Kiera suggested quietly as they debated this. "Both Kent and the headmaster are master magicians. The magic might tip them off to our location. Plus, if Kent is evil—"

There was the sound of footsteps approaching the door from inside the office and they all froze. The door handle started to turn and Kiera heard Tucker utter a spell under his breath a second before the door opened.

They all froze as Kent took one step into the hall. They were crouching five feet away, pressed against the wall but still in plain sight. Kiera held her breath as the man's steeled eyes drifted over them. He couldn't see them! Tucker must have cast an invisibility spell at the last second.

Kent hesitated a moment longer, his face morphing into a scowl, then he turned back into the office. "We'll discuss this later. Just rest assured that I'm not lying about Ezra. He went home to his family for reasons we want to keep private, even from extended relatives like you." He emphasized the word extended to emphasize that this wasn't the headmaster's business. "This is your last warning to stay out of it, *Charles*."

Kiera bristled at how cold his voice had become. She always knew his smiling teacher aura was an act, but the difference here was like black and white.

All three of them stiffened again as Kent shut the door behind him, then walked down the hall. He brushed past them, mere inches from their knees, and Kiera feared a mere breath would alert him to where they were.

He was almost past when he paused again and turned slightly.

Kiera was tempted to close her eyes like she did in scary dreams but didn't. Then Kent turned and looked right at her, the right side of his mouth quirking upwards.

He could see them. They'd been caught. She was right. They shouldn't have used magic when dealing with such skilled magicians.

Kent raised his hand before any of them could make a move. It wouldn't have mattered if they screamed anyway. Ben's silence spell was still up. Shouting out would only ring inside their own heads, deafening them. Kiera didn't have time to think of a proper spell to use against Kent anyway. Who knew what kind of counters he had planned to defend himself.

As his fingers lifted into the air, Kiera felt the

floor underneath her give way. She was so in awe of his ability to cast a spell without speaking a word that it took her an extra second to realize she had left the staff building in the blink of an eye and was now crouching in a forest clearing. They had teleported. There were no buildings in sight, though the slightly off colors of the foliage around her told her she was still on the university grounds.

Kent, Ben, and Tucker were still with her, crouching like they were a moment ago. Kent had transported all of them into the forest. He probably did it because a teleport spell wouldn't tip off the headmaster. An attack spell would, or a memory-altering spell as Kiera was now sure she had done to them in the past, but transport generally shouldn't raise any alarms.

"You're the one who erased our memories!" Ben shouted, finally leaping to his feet and letting his voice run free again. "You erased Kiera's boyfriend!" His shout was quickly followed by an attack spell that sent a ball of fire right at Kent.

Kiera got to her feet too as Kent stepped out of the path of the blazing ball of flame, sending it flying toward the tree behind him. He raised his hand before it could light the entire forest on fire and cast a spell that made it fizzle out. Just as Kiera suspected, Kent was using far-higher levels spells than Ben was, making it nearly impossible to touch him.

As Tucker cast a shield spell around them, Kiera felt her own magic swirl around her, aching for a fight. For once, she would give it to them. She opened her mouth to utter a necromancy death spell on Kent and found that the words flowed fast and clear despite how nervous she was. A year of constant practice had finally paid off in a tense situation.

Kent turned toward her, his eyes glinting with amusement, and as she uttered the last word of the spell, he grinned. The last word from her lips was meant to make him drop dead, or at the very least knock him unconscious, but all it did was make his smile widen.

"You really thought you could use death magic on a head necromancer," Kent asked her with a chuckle. "If you weren't so useful, I would deflect your death spell back at you in a heartbeat."

Useful? Kiera glanced at Ben and Tucker, who looked equally unsure how to fight this man. They didn't know high enough level spells to counter him. Maybe Ezra would have but he wasn't here.

Wait! She just had a thought about the Ezra person. The thought had come naturally, like muscle memory recalling something even when her mind didn't. The memory spell must have some cracks in it. This specific thought about Ezra wasn't helpful in the moment, but that meant even if Kent erased their memories again, it wouldn't work perfectly.

"What are you planning to do to us?" Tucker asked, clearly stalling with his calm voice and tone. Ben was muttering another spell but Kiera knew whatever it was wouldn't work.

"I'm glad you asked that, Tucker," Kent said stepping closer and passing right through the shield Tucker had set up to protect the three of them. "Because I was hoping to take this time to explain my evil plan."

Ben shouted the last word in the foreign language spells used and a black ball of flame sped toward Kent before fizzling out and disappearing like a popped bubble. The failure made Ben shout like a child having a tantrum, which only made Kent's smile get even wider and more unnatural.

"Seriously, though," Kent said, studying each of them. "What were you doing at the headmaster's office? Did you figure out what I did to you?"

"Don't say anything," Ben's voice came into Kiera's head. "He's trying to make his next spell foolproof."

"I can hear that," Kent said.

Ben's face turned red with rage. "How?" he muttered under his breath, cursing Kent's skills.

Kent smirked again. "Join the classes I teach with Kiera and a few others and you can find out. I'm not a bad man. I just know you and your magic are being held back by all these rules and limitations. I want to help others reach their potential. That's all I've ever wanted, even for someone like Charles."

"What did you do to Ezra?" Kiera asked. She wasn't even furious about their gaps in skill. Her heart still remembered her boyfriend and she wanted him back. If even the headmaster, who was related to Ezra, didn't know where he was, Kent *must* have done something to him.

"I could tell you, since I'm about to erase your memories," Kent said casually as he moved his hands around oddly, his fingers cracking unnaturally as he prepared some spell. "But since the last attempt at the spell didn't work out as I hoped, I'm not taking any chances by explaining everything to you."

"Why erase our memories if you're not even confident in your own spells?" Tucker asked, trying to trick the man into revealing himself. Sadly, Kent gave him a look that let him know he was onto him.

"Teenagers," he said, sighing dramatically.

"Always convincing themselves they're smarter than adults. I'm not some mustache-twirling villain who is going to let you walk all over me. None of you were supposed to get involved. I want it to stay that way. As soon as this spell ends, I want you three to just go about your lives, date, study, graduate, get jobs, and leave without looking back. This is for your own good. Be glad I'm under someone else's rule. If I had it my way, I'd kill you all here and now."

"And what about Ezra?" Kiera countered, unwilling to let him skip over that point. "He deserves to live a normal life too."

Kent turned to her again. His eyes were so empty and soulless that it made both her and the magic around her go cold. It looked like he hated this Ezra person so much that he no longer felt anything but mindless rage toward him. "If he never existed, *I* could have lived the normal life I just described. He has already taken my dreams and future away. Don't let him take yours too."

"That's not for you to decide!" Kiera shouted but Kent wasn't listening to her anymore. He had turned away and his hands were outstretched, each finger pointing awkwardly at the three of them. For a brief moment, his eyes looked completely black and Kiera got a sense of strong déjà vu.

Then, there was a bright flash. The ground disappeared from under her again.

She was back in her dorm room. Wait. Back? She'd been in this room all day. Hadn't she? It was nearly noon. Why had she been cooped up in here all day?

Kiera pressed both hands to her head, feeling woozy. Her mind was all fuzzy, like she'd had a horrible nap and had just woken up mid-dream. This felt awful, and that sense of being pulled was tugging on her again, urging her to go downwards.

What just happened? She didn't feel like herself today. It was like she'd zoned out all morning and had just come to her senses. The magic around her was all tense too, like it had just been used and was only now calming down.

None of this felt right. Something bad was happening right under her nose and she needed to figure out what it was. That, or she needed to leave this campus forever. The longer she stayed in this school, the more cursed it felt. She was beginning to wish she'd stayed at a non-magical school after all.

❧ 5 ❧

During the rest of the winter break, Kiera noticed a few more strange things going on besides the strange morning she had on that one day and the weird tugging toward the ground, but she mostly brushed them off as nerves from graduation or from the gargoyle attacks last semester. Sure, there was a constant sense of dread in the back of her mind now and the feeling of losing something or someone important, but that could just be tension and anxiety warping her mind. After all, she needed to eventually apply to medical magician schools and that was a stressful ordeal. There was also the worry that maybe medicine wasn't the right career path. It was so hard to get into Dreadmore Academy, after all, so it felt like a waste to leave after only two years spent here.

Maybe becoming a doctor wasn't for her. Maybe she'd hate the job.

That was why she dove into her studies yet again during this free time. Ben would sometimes ask her if she felt weird like he did and he'd occasionally convince her to scour the grounds for anything suspicious, but she only did it to humor him. She already had too much anxiety from school. No need to add onto it. Tucker the same as her. He was nervous and couldn't understand why, but he had school and family to focus on. Ben was the only one who didn't obsess over grades and his future, so that explained why he was more willing to worry over unimportant, irrational fears.

"You're telling me you *really* don't feel any different from last semester?" Ben asked one day during their final week of holidays. They were seated in the nearly empty library, with Kiera and Tucker pouring over next semester's textbooks while Ben had an unopened comic book resting on his lap. "I'm telling you, something fishy is going on around here and I want to figure out what it is."

"If something is wrong, the faculty will figure it out," Tucker said quietly, clearly annoyed from the distraction.

"Oh yeah, like they've done for the last two years. They're *so* reliable," Ben answered grumpily.

"Why don't you text Meiying instead of bothering us?" Kiera asked, getting annoyed too.

Ben had done nothing but rant about feeling strange and uncomfortable for a full week now and she'd grown tired of it. What made it worse was she felt the same way but knew there was nothing they could do about it. It was normal for students entering adulthood to be nervous. Ben just wasn't dealing with it in a mature manner. That was totally normal for him, but Kiera was reaching her breaking point with him today.

"I'm going to study outside," she said, grabbing her books and standing up before they could stop her.

"It's getting colder out there," Tucker warned her as she headed out. Even though there was some kind of environmental spell over the campus that made everything more like spring and fall combined, rather than straight up winter, the breeze still brought a chill with it.

"I'll use a warmth spell if I need it," Kiera replied, eager to leave before she got fed up and said some harsh things to Ben that she'd later regret. She really did want to get through this current textbook chapter, so a change of environment would be good for her.

"Be careful," Ben called after her as she exited.

"Don't let your guard down around here."

Way to make her feel better. *Thanks a lot, Ben.*

She didn't end up using a heat spell as she traversed the grounds. The wind wasn't blowing today. The only hint that it was there at all was the slight hiss of it passing between buildings that were too close together. Even that sound died down as she left the tall buildings and concrete paths of the school and entered the forest behind it. A few birds flitted past, their feathers an unnaturally bright purple, but none of them attacked her as Ben had implied they might. He'd been acting like the whole campus was out to get them lately. She wanted to say she couldn't understand why he was so on edge, but she knew why because she felt the same way. Something had changed since winter break began and it hadn't reverted back to normal in the last week.

Her textbook felt heavier the longer she walked, and if she didn't know any better, she felt like gravity was getting stronger too. Once again, that now familiar ache to descend past the dirt and into the Earth's core was strengthening. It was tugging her back toward the buildings, though, and grew more insistent the farther away she wandered.

"I wonder if I should follow the pull," she muttered, partly to herself and partly to the magic she was aware flitted around her. The magic felt lighter whenever she was in nature, like it belonged here as much as humans did.

She had refused to follow this persistent tugging up until now, though she'd considered giving in several times. The only thing holding her back was the fear that it was some type of trap, like the light of an anglerfish luring in prey.

It took a few minutes of thought to come to a decision. The trees lured her in, telling her to sit down and rest in nature, but the tug continued, like an ever-present pulse in her spine. If she didn't follow it now, she might never get a chance. The campus would fill up with students again a week from now and then she'd have less room to roam freely. However, she'd also feel safer if there were more people about. Which pro outweighed the other?

Finally, she gave in and headed back toward the campus buildings, this time following the pulse and ignoring the hairs rising on the back of her neck. Curiosity had led her to the fairy door last year, but she'd been less skilled in magic back then. Now, her connection to the magic around her was stronger than ever. It had protected her in the past without the need of a vocal spell. She was confident it would save her if there was a real threat around.

Once she reached the gardens at the back of the campus, she became confident that she was on the right path. Not only did the tugging get loosen and relax, but her emotions moved along with it. The emptiness inside her dulled.

Once she was back in the middle of the campus, next to the school's fountain connecting the paths leading to all the different buildings, she put her hand on the cold ground and tried to feel what was calling to her beneath it. The snow crystals wet her warm hand and she felt the magic moving around her palm. There was a strong sense of life beneath the ground, pulsing like a heart beat, but with that strange sense of life came an ominous feeling of death. It reminded her of screams and blood. The sense of torment became so strong that she had to pull her bare hand away in surprise.

Something evil was beneath her, but she couldn't comprehend what it was or why it was below them. She also couldn't understand why it called out specifically to *her*. Ben and Tucker said they didn't feel the same thing when she asked them. They just felt off. There was no tug for them. Why was she different?

She was still trying to wrap her head around it when someone called out to her.

"Kiera! I was just looking for you!" It was

Professor Gillis, her homeroom teacher. He was approaching her with a smile and raised hand, waving at her from the necromancy building. "I wanted to discuss our special classes before they started up again."

Right. She'd been taking some extra necromancy classes that only a few other students attended. Professor Gillis didn't look too happy about it. Something must have happened to the classes. Maybe he lost permission to continue or the budget was cut.

"Since you're one of my most promising students, I wanted to assure you that the classes are still continuing," he told her as he got closer. "But a few of the students let me know they were dropping out. I think the holidays have reminded them how nice a lack of extra classes can be," he joked.

"Oh." Kiera could tell he was planning to ask if she wanted to drop out too. Luckily, she didn't mind the extra education. She needed all the help she could get. "I still plan to come."

"Oh, good." He looked relieved. "I was thinking of inviting a few more students to make up for those we lost, so I wanted to ask if you prefer a smaller class or a larger one. I know some students prefer the more personal, smaller groups."

Kiera shrugged. "I don't particularly care either

way." If she was being honest, she barely remembered what she learned in the classes, nor who she shared them with. "Small groups make me more comfortable," she added when it was clear the non-answer wasn't enough to satisfy him.

"Excellent. In that case, I'll get a bit more feedback and leave it small if all the other students agree. We had five students drop out, so it'll just be the ten of you remaining. I'll see how everyone else feels."

"Okay." Kiera wasn't sure why he was bringing this up. He wasn't exactly her favorite teacher and she knew he didn't consider her his top student. "Was there anything else you needed?"

"Not particularly." He looked down at the handprint she had left in the snow beneath their feet. "I was wondering why you were touching the ground like that, though."

"Oh." She felt the back of her neck heat up, embarrassed from getting caught. He was studying her, analyzing her like she'd gone crazy. Maybe she had. "I just thought I saw something in the snow and wanted to check. I used to enjoy searching for lost coins on the ground as a child so..." she lied, trying not to gulp nervously and make herself look guilty.

"Oh," he said, his true reaction masked. "That's

funny. You won't need to stress about money anymore, though. High level magicians rarely need to worry about any human necessities. Food and clothing can be easily brought in with a spell."

"Right." Kiera forced a laugh to satisfy him, then took a step back toward the library. That feeling of underground death already had her on edge and Professor Gillis wasn't helping. "Well, see you next week."

"Until then. I look forward to teaching you all sorts of weird and wonderful spells!" He waved at her but when she turned to walk back to the library, she thought she saw his smile falter for a second when he thought her back was turned. Maybe she should have turned down his extra classes after all. No, that would be a bad idea. Just because the teacher was a little odd didn't mean she should give up a chance to learn more about necromancy. Professor Gillis was a very skilled magician. He could teach her a lot of useful and exciting spells that other teachers wouldn't. Even though her gut told her something was off, she didn't let that hamper her excitement for this last semester. She had to cram in as much knowledge as possible before the medical school took over. Without a set career, her future would look pretty bleak, especially since she'd be going into it alone.

6

Nothing else of note happened over the holidays. Ben became a little insufferable with how nervous he became, which wasn't like him, and Tucker ended up hanging out by himself rather than with Ben and Kiera since he wanted to focus on studying. Kiera managed to pick up some extra medical spells during her free time but her anticipation for the extra necromancy classes was building. Despite her nerves—from both Ben and the creepy death feeling underground—her curiosity about magic stayed strong. That was why, after all the students returned and the next semester's classes began on Monday, she was excited for regular classes to end.

The afternoon trek downstairs to the extra class in the necromancy building was just as eerie as ever.

The stone walls were moist and imposing, the darkness crowded around her, the silence was suffocating, and there was a constant urge to look over her shoulder. However, once she reached the wooden door leading into the classroom and saw the roaring fireplace, its warmth brought a bit of much needed comfort.

Professor Gillis was seated in front of fifteen empty chairs, his legs crossed and head tilted to the side as he patiently waited for his students to arrive. Since Kiera was still a little scared of him, she took a seat at the far end of the row, as far from him as she could be. Sadly, since she was the only one here, he turned his attention to her immediately. She shouldn't have come so early.

"I'm glad you came," he told her. "I know I said this before, Kiera, but I mean it when I say potentially you are one of the most powerful members of this class."

"Thank you," she said awkwardly, not sure how to react to such sudden praise.

"You may not believe me now, since you're still a beginner, but most people have a limit on what level of spells they can use. Anything too high drains them of energy, then eventually life. You and I aren't like that. Our limit on magic is far higher. While that isn't particularly rare in a magic user, it's still impressive and rarely utilized properly." He folded his hands on his lap, smiling at her like a proud parent. "Growing up, I met a lot of students who weren't taught properly or were held back. I want to help you avoid that. I see your potential and want to help you use it to its fullest extent."

"Huh." Kiera nodded, gulping. She had no response to that. "I'm excited to learn more," she said dully.

"That's what I like to hear." He thankfully didn't say more as other students started entering and choosing a seat. She recognized most of them from the earlier classes but there were a few new kids as well. Most of them looked ecstatic about being included in these classes. It almost felt like an exclusive club that you needed to specially qualify for. In a way, it was true.

"I'm glad everyone's here," Professor Gillis, Kent, said. "I'm sorry that some of you will fall behind in the beginning, but rest assured, you'll catch up quickly. However, before we begin, I'd like to preface that the spells we will be learning take a while to adjust to—mentally, that is. Learning too much at once, especially magic, can overwhelm one's brain, so at the end of each class, your memory will be temporarily erased."

There were a few murmurs from the newcomers

and Kiera was struck with a strong sense of unease, but no one protested.

"You'll remember everything that was erased when you return to this class next time, and by the end of the semester, I'll return everything you were taught to your conscious brain. However, just know that you will leave this room and not remember. That's okay. Don't panic. If you have any questions, feel free to ask now or later and I'll be happy to help walk you through the process. I'll also remind you of this when you exit the classroom today."

Now that he had mentioned memory loss and the lessons, her own memories of the classes was coming back. She vaguely recalled learning about resurrection and entering the spirit world. She also remembered being creeped out by both those things back then but now it didn't seem so strange. They were necromancers. Death was part of life. Instead of running from death, necromancers utilized it to do good. She wasn't sure why her past self made such a big deal of Professor Gillis's lessons.

The spirit world, as far as she recalled, wasn't that bad either. It was just a place where you could see other spirits. There was one thing about it she couldn't remember, though. What was it she'd forgotten?

"Sir?" she asked.

Professor Gillis had already started answering questions and she'd been zoning out so she missed most of them.

"Call me Kent."

"Right. Kent." It felt familiar to call him by his first name, which was odd. She couldn't recall doing it before. "I remember entering the spirit world, but can we review how to get out again."

"Oh, that's right." Kent nodded, recognition lighting his eyes... as well as something else Kiera couldn't decipher. "I helped you leave the spirit world last time. I'll have to teach all of you to do it on your own eventually. Don't worry. That will come later, once you are experienced with entering the world first. I'll be coming with you until you've mastered the exit."

That was a relief. Kiera would hate to get trapped in there. She recalled it being an interesting place, filled with colorful lights that represented people's souls, but no one would want to stay there forever.

"Since you seem eager," Kent said, turning toward Kiera and making all the other students do the same, "Would you like to go first, Kiera?"

Anxiety shot up her arms but she kept her expression neutral. "Sure." She was eager to get back in there and figure out if this gut feeling was wrong. If the teacher came with her, there should be no risk too, right? After all, if entering that realm was dangerous, it would killed her the last time she went.

"Excellent." Kent flashed her a toothy smile and gestured for her to go ahead. "Everyone pay attention because you'll be going next."

Kiera took a deep breath, then started the spell Kent had taught her. She could feel her magic zipping around her, then traveling right inside her body. There was a sense of magical movement from Kent too. He must be casting either the same spell or a protective one.

Everyone held their breath as she continued. Then, just like before, she felt herself fall through the floor.

ntering the spirit world felt much easier this time around. Before, it felt draining and required either a lot of concentration or help from someone else. Now, it almost felt natural. The dip through the floor didn't feel as scary and disorienting. One second she was falling, the next she was standing in darkness and her eyes were adjusting quickly to the misty location she had entered.

If there was anything different about the spirit world, she didn't notice it right off the bat. There were fourteen small colorful orbs sitting next to her. They must belong to the students. Kent's spirit was the only one she couldn't see, though she could *feel* it nearby, prodding her forward. He must be watching over her. Good. His presence made her feel less alone in here.

Despite her mind telling her everything was okay and she'd be leaving in a minute or two, the hairs on the back of her now non-existent neck were still standing up. Her legs felt wobbly too, though when she looked down, she could no longer see them.

Once again, the feeling from the hallway that she needed to look over her shoulder returned. However, this time, she felt less silly about giving in. Holding her breath, she looked over her shoulder and saw—nothing. She was alone, with only the orbs beside her. So why did she feel like there was something, or someone, watching her from behind?

The feeling of being pulled was present too, though this time it pulled her forward and backward at the same time, rather than down.

"Is someone there?" she whispered, listening to her voice echo. It sounded dull, like she was in a vacuum. "Hello?"

No answer.

Just like how she could now feel her own magic around her, she could feel some more spirits or souls in here with her too. Kent wasn't the only one present. There were others too, both behind and in front of her form.

She paused to feel the direction of the tug, then acknowledged that it was pulling her forward. Maybe it was a good idea to follow it.

She took a step, feeling like gravity no longer existed, and with each step, the pull got stronger, like it was desperate to suck her in. Had the tugging she'd felt in the real world been trying to bring her *here* all along? Into the spirit world?

"Kiera," a voice whispered, drifting around her like the mist. It sounded neither male nor female and was hissing, more akin to a snake than a human. "Kiera."

She held back the will to shriek and stopped moving. This was wrong.

"Kiera," it whispered again, getting louder.

"What are you?" she whispered. No answer. "*Where* are you?"

"Kiera," it said again, whispering right into her ear.

Kiera turned, terrified, and saw nothing but dark trails of mist wisping around her.

Her breathing quickened. She should have asked Kent how to leave before entering. She wanted to leave right now!

"Kent!" she shouted, stepping back and away from where the voice was last. "I want to leave!"

No answer from him.

Next she heard an inhuman shriek behind her head. It made her entire being shake and she tried to shut her eyes but couldn't. It felt like her body, or rather her soul, was being drained of energy from the fear.

"Kent!" she shouted again, looking around and seeing no one. She couldn't even feel Kent's presence anymore. The tug was still persistent, urging her forward, but it might belong to this shrieking, whispering thing so she couldn't trust it anymore. "Help me!"

The shriek stopped and the silence became even worse—oppressive and driving home the sense that something was creeping up on her.

Then she heard her name one more time, right next to her ear, and it was accompanied by a physical breath.

"Come here," it whispered, its voice moist and evil and with a bit of the shriek still within it, making Kiera believe that if death could speak, it would sound like this. "Kiera."

Then, finally, Kiera fell through the floor again.

She was back in the room, hyperventilating and being stared at by the other students. Her hands were shaking as she pressed her forehead against her legs, trying to regain control of her body and lungs. The shriek was still echoing in her ears. She couldn't go back there. Whatever was in that world wanted to kill her. The tug had been a trap all along, just as she suspected.

"Are you okay, Kiera?" Kent asked calmly, seeming unaware of what she'd just experienced. "We can take a break if it was too overwhelming. I had assumed it would be okay for you to go in first since you'd gone several times before."

"I'm okay," she choked, unsure if she should tell him the truth or not. "But I don't want to go in again. Not yet." No wonder she'd felt dread about entering. She should have listened to her heart rather than her brain.

"I completely understand. The voices of souls, especially lost or angry ones, can be frightening. However, rest assured that I will never let anything harm you in there," Kent said, addressing both her and the other students. "I have complete control. Eventually, all of you will learn to wield that control as well."

Yes, she wanted control. If this tugging toward the spirit world was going to become a permanent thing, she wanted to at least have a weapon to use against it. She just hoped Kent would help with that, as he said, rather than make things worse. Maybe his introduction to this other realm had brought things into Kiera's life that he shouldn't have and now she had no way to get rid of it.

"I want to assure you, Kiera," Kent added, quieter this time. "Your magic is very powerful. You are one of the most capable people to enter this realm and survive. Believe in yourself. Don't let the fear convince you to give up."

She nodded, knowing she was already in too deep and wanting to conquer this. A part of her still wished she had never entered that world in the first place. IgKierance was bliss and she missed never knowing about all the things lurking right beside her, always present but never observed. If whatever had tried to lure her in the spirit world could enter the real one, Kiera doubted Kent could control it.

$$\approx \quad 8 \quad \approx$$

"Someone else was in there with us," Kiera told Kent after the class ended. She managed to corner him before he left and wanted to know exactly what was going on in that spirit world. "Who was it?"

"Do you mean the souls?" he asked, then described the orbs accurately. "The color supposedly refers to the personality and morals, though that's just a theory some people have. You don't need to worry about those. Only we can interact with them. They can't harm us."

"No, not the souls," Kiera whispered, clenching her hands together at the memory. "There was someone or something else in there with me, with us. I don't think it had good intentions." That or it was just horrible at socializing.

Kent frowned. "Can you give me more details? I don't recall anyone else being in this part of the realm when you entered. I checked beforehand."

Kiera wished she could cast a truthfulness spell on him at that moment, since he was so hard to read, but she knew he'd realize right away and stop her. "I felt like there were one or two people behind me, and at least one of them spoke to me, calling my name. There were other people there too... I think. I don't know how many there were or where they were standing. I just felt the urge to get closer to them."

Kent looked deep in thought. "Maybe your consciousness of magic and spirits is higher than mine. I can assure you, there was no one else with us. I have heard of people going a little mad when they enter the spirit realm. It's akin to schizophrenia, creating hallucinations. Maybe we shouldn't let you back in just yet. Perhaps a therapist would help—"

"No!" She knew she wasn't going crazy. They were really there, she was sure of it. She felt like she'd at least seen or heard the two figures behind her in the past too. The memory was fuzzy but there. "I'm fine," she added when he gave her a funny look. "I just want to know what I'm getting myself into... and if it's safe."

"It is," he assured her, then patted her on the shoulder. "Let's discuss this next time. Keep practicing your magic and work on the spells related to spirits as well, though you should never enter the spirit realm without my help."

No promises there. He might be hiding something from her. "You'll erase my memory of how to do it once I leave the room anyway, right?"

"Right."

Fantastic. "Until next time, then."

She could feel Kent's eyes on her back as she left. It felt like he was analyzing her. Maybe he genuinely thought she was going nuts.

As soon as she stepped through the door, she felt her brain go fuzzy for thirty seconds, then the memory of what she'd learned today drifted away. The jittery-ness and raised hairs on her body remained, though, so she knew something bad had happened. The curiosity was still there too and she knew it was related to both death and the tug she had felt for the past three weeks. She knew she'd have to come back for the next class, as well as figure out what this tug was pulling her toward. Hopefully it wouldn't end up killing her in the process. Curiosity killed the cat. Mystery killed the magician. One could only hope Kiera wouldn't fall into those categories too.

She went to sleep a little nervous. She wasn't the type to sleep with a night light but when every sound made her sit up and search for a monster or intruder, she had to create one with a long-term spell that would keep going even when she went to sleep. Then she put some extra locks and force-fields around her before finally feeling at peace, enough to fall asleep at least.

Sadly, her dreams were what she should have been worried about, not reality. As soon as she drifted off, she found herself back in an even creepier version of the spirit realm, but this time there wasn't just a voice down there. There was a real figure attached to it this time.

The first things she saw when she entered sleep was darkness, then the mist, then the little glowing orbs. All of them were a deep red or dark grey now, rather than the pretty colors she saw in reality. They cast an eerie glow on everything, including her limbs which she could now see in this dream version of the realm. She almost wished she didn't have a body. At least then she would feel invincible.

The whispering, hissing voice from before came again, though this time it was a mix of her mother's voice and something demonic she would have heard in a horror film. It whistled around her head, taunting her for coming back here and describing the horrible things it planned to do to her.

"Use your magic," it told her after it finished explaining all the horrid things it could do. "Kill me. Burn me. Destroy me."

Why would it want her to use magic on it? This felt like a test or trap. She hated it.

Ignoring the voice and refusing to do what it wanted, she started walking forward, away from it. The tug that had become more of a familiar pulse led her forward. This time it felt like she could actually reach it. Was it real or was it just part of the dream?

She knew something was following her—she could hear its pounding footsteps and many feet making soft thumps behind her—but she ignored it. Looking at it would only make it more real and maybe then it could make good on its threats. She wouldn't give it the satisfaction.

Finally, the pulse was so strong and weak at the same time that she was sure she was only a few feet away from its source. Only then did she see something else that wasn't the horrid creature. There was another form in front of her, one only slightly taller than her. It was cloaked in shadow but she could feel a warm familiarity about it. It almost felt the same as her magic, which had become so comfortable and ever-present that she enjoyed having it around. This thing, or person, felt the same.

"Who are you?" she whispered to the figure, its human body outlined by the slight red and grey glow behind it. "Why have you been pulling me toward you?"

The figure turned toward her but its face and body didn't become any clearer.

They both stood there for a moment, her breaths labored and mind afraid to move lest she scare the person off.

Then it lifted its head, as though looking at something behind and above her. It must see whatever had been following her. Should she look up too?

Before she could decide, the comforting figure reached forward and grabbed her hand. She could tell the things wrapping around her wrist were human fingers, but they were so cold they had to be dead. That made her nearly pull away. She looked down, trying to get a better look at the darkened thing's hand, but then she awoke and all the sensations vanished, replaced by the warm, scratchy feeling of a blanket on her skin. They grey and red lights were replaced by the singular yellow one she had placed in the corner of the room to serve as a makeshift nightlight. There were no more creatures breathing down her neck, nor a cold hand gripping hers as though its life depended on not letting go.

However, something in the room had changed. The thing or person's hand might be gone from hers, but she could still feel its presence with her. It was like it rested on the bed right beside her, present but invisible. It didn't feel threatening or intimidating—it was just there. The being felt comforting too, like having a dog sleep next to you and guard you. Even though she didn't know who or what it was, she felt relieved it was there. Maybe she should have followed the tug after all, back when the holidays started. It might be a trap, but her gut told her it wasn't. It was just a nice presence that had been calling out to her all this time.

She went back to sleep and never felt the presence leave during that night. Her dreams were empty this time, mercifully blank for one night.

9

Kiera didn't tell Ben and Tucker about the presence following her around. She worried it would drive the already paranoid Ben over the edge and Tucker would start casting spells on it to figure out what it was. That might scare it away. She just tried to treat it like she did the ever-growing magic that always followed her around. This thing was distinctly different from that—the flitting, jittery magic was more like a wind whereas this being felt solid with real hands and feet to carry it along—but she pretended it was the same so it wouldn't creep her out or make her get too casual around it.

There was still a chance it was a trap or a spy or some other dark creature from the spirit realm that was meant to stay there, but she enjoyed having it around so much that she couldn't bear to investigate it or scare it away.

This strange presence, and the peace that came with it, was the cause of her shift in focus and energies. Throughout the coming month, she found herself enjoying the secret classes with Kent more and more. What she could recall of those classes, which was very little, was the excitement of entering a new world bordering their own. She and the other students would always exit the classroom in its eerie hallway filled with a sense of wonder. There was also a bit of condescension growing within them, she felt, at the knowledge that they were able to access something most magic users couldn't. They were like archeologists or explorers, charting new territory that they could one day show to the world upon graduation.

Even though Kiera would sometimes exit the classes feeling a bit tired and drained, as though she'd just run a marathon without lifting a finger, the chills from seeing something new and powerful always overcame it. Soon, that dull ache and burn of passion overpowered her other classes. When she was sitting through a normal class, her thoughts drifted to the tiny bits and pieces she recalled from Kent's, sticking them together like an puzzle without all the pieces. It was like a mystery to be solved, what they were doing in there. She could feel it strengthening her magic and bringing more of it in, or at least making the magic she currently had bigger. She was immensely curious as to what was causing the increase.

Her studies went from learning new spells and reading textbooks to solely studying necromancy, or rather the history of it and how to access banned, forbidden works about it. She needed to figure out what Kent was teaching them and then hiding from them. She had to know what it was that was leaving her so excited and dreadful after each class. Whatever it was, she wanted to do it now, rather than just whenever Kent was around. The sense of wonder and mystery was eating away at her.

One other thing was starting to drive her obsession around necromancy and entering whatever world it was they were accessing. The strange presence she had felt alongside her magic was growing stronger and more real every time she finished her secret classes. To add to that, she could feel other presences starting to join it. Some felt innocent and helpful like that first one, while others felt suspicious and unwelcome. Whatever she was doing in that other realm was tethering them to her and she wasn't sure if she wanted even more to latch on, not until she knew exactly what they were, at least.

Thanks to this new obsession and the drain on her body that was sapping away all her energy, her grades started to drop. This wasn't anything new, since she'd always struggled to keep her grades up, but since she was so close to applying to medical schools, she kept the news hidden from her parents. If this drop had been a result of things she couldn't control, like a too-high difficulty or illness, she wouldn't feel embarrassed, but because it was her own distracting obsession to blame, she didn't want her mom to know about it. That would lead to them figuring out she was attending extra classes that were exhausting her, and that in turn would lead to them forbidding her to go. She didn't want that. Then she'd never learn how she was entering this other world and what it even was. The mystery would haunt her forever, taunting her with knowledge just out of her reach.

So, she kept going to Kent's special classes, kept ignoring her regular ones, kept becoming weakened and latched on to, and refused to stop. Even when her magic started feeling like it was being pulled away from something, or used by something else, she didn't stop. She had to see this through.

There was also a nagging feeling that this persistent tugging on her soul, which was still present despite that first spirit or whatever it was joining her, might be answered by Kent's lessons at some point. She'd tried to follow the tugging at numerous points but was never able to find the true source of the pull. It always told her to go deeper, underground, and there wasn't any spell she could use that would let her safely do that. She was sure the tug was related to the spirit realm they were entering, so once Kent deemed her ready and gave her back her memories, she'd be able to finally figure out what it was.

Needless to say, all these jumbled emotions and wants led to her looking exhausted, gaunt, and sleepy at almost every hour. Alongside her grades dropping, her appetite fell and her weight started going down alongside it. Her parents couldn't tell, since they only spoke on the phone, but there was one other person close to her who could see it happening: Ben.

And he didn't plan to sit by and watch as she tore herself apart for a little mysterious magic.

10

Kiera entered the cafeteria late for dinner. It was a Wednesday, near the start of February, and Sally had already left their table because it was getting late. Darkness had already descended over the grounds so Kiera didn't blame her for not waiting up. Kiera had been too busy walking around the grounds, hunting for some secret passage that would take her underground so she could follow the pull. She'd made a habit of it but always came up empty.

She looked awful as she walked up to the corner table where her friends sat. Ben and Meiying were next to each other, their plates nearly empty, and Tucker was seated across from them, reading a book about magic shields as he bit into an apple for dessert. They all looked clean and rested, while Kiera's boots were muddy and her skin pale.

"You look awful," Ben commented bluntly as she placed her tray of pork, spinach, and boiled potatoes on the table. "Like when..." He paused, as though forgetting what he was about to say, or who he was about to compare her to. "Where were you?" he asked instead, cutting off his previous train of thought. "We haven't seen you all day."

"Studying," she lied coldly, not wanting to talk about it.

Tucker glanced at her, probably detecting the lie. They all knew her grades weren't doing too well. Second years had access to a leader board, so they knew her tests had gone poorly.

"No you weren't," Ben said, not willing to act subtle like Meiying or polite like Tucker. "Stop lying to me. We all know something's wrong with you. I mean, look at you." He gestured at her tight skin and pale coloring. "You look half dead."

"Not my fault. Maybe I came down with something," Kiera evaded. She didn't even know the full answer. She suspected whatever Kent was teaching her had been draining her, but since most of her memories of those classes faded quickly, she couldn't answer what the true cause was.

"I think Kent's up to something," Ben said. "I can feel it. We all can."

"Ben," Tucker said, tired. "We've been over this. There's no evidence. You're just paranoid and don't like him."

"No! Don't shut me down again. He's up to something. I get a bad feeling every time I see him with Kiera. Plus, there's that gap in our memories that—"

"Again with the memories?" Kiera asked, unsure why Ben was so obsessed with bringing up memories. It's not like *he* was taking Kent's class and having his memories wiped. Why did he keep pretending his own memories had been wiped too. "Just give it a rest, Ben. Nothing is out to get us."

"See! That's strange too!" Ben pointed at both Kiera and Tucker accusingly. "None of you are acting like yourselves. You're always out of it and trying to convince yourselves there is no danger. It's like someone's cast a spell on you."

"If someone's cast a spell on us," Tucker said, "Why didn't they cast it on you too? What makes you so special?"

"I'm not special. I'm just not willing to give up like you two are. Tucker, you've never been this nonchalant about everything and unwilling to investigate things. That used to be my job. And Kiera, you look like a walking corpse and you don't even care. You're so obsessed with those special classes you take and aren't even a little bit worried that the teacher keeps erasing your memories. For all we know, Kent could be torturing you down there and you wouldn't even know—"

"I would know. I would have marks on my body, wouldn't I?" Kiera sighed. "I'm tired of fighting, Ben. This is the first semester we've had where nothing is going wrong. Why can't you just let the peace continue?"

"Because there is no peace!" Ben slammed his fist on the table, making Meiying jump. She moved her hand to stop him and calm him down but he was ignoring her. His glare never left Tucker and Kiera's faces. "Something is wrong here, with both this school and you two. What's worse is I know something like this happened to us before and we didn't do anything about it back then too."

Tucker frowned. "Nothing like this has happened before—"

"It has! I can feel it."

More eye rolls from both Tucker and Kiera. They'd had to hear Ben's rants about his "déjà vu" and "feelings" all month. It was getting old.

"Why don't you just go read your comic books

and procrastinate like you used to?" Kiera grumbled. "Stop worrying about Kent or me or whatever."

Kiera saw a flicker of hurt flash through Ben's eyes. She was making fun of how he used to never care about anything. Back when they were kids, he would barely study and cared more about videogames than people. Now that he was finally learning to care, they were pushing him out.

Kiera felt a sting of guilt for pushing away her lifelong friend, but he was trying to make her doubt the one thing that gave her a sense of purpose. If she quit attending Kent's classes, she'd have nothing to do with her life. She was single with mediocre grades and little passion for anything besides magic. Without these mysteries to solve and realms to explore, she had nothing. Ben couldn't understand. He'd always naturally been smart and he had a girlfriend he loved. He lacked nothing and listening to him try to tear apart Kiera's focus was like having his accomplishments rubbed in her face.

She knew her cruelty toward him was wrong. She was just shoving her own insecurities and inadequacies onto him, but she was too tired and angry at him right now to care.

Kiera cringed as Ben got up from the table,

refusing to look at her now. She'd made her position abundantly clear.

"Don't trust Kent," he said before leaving. "And don't trust yourselves anymore. I don't think any of us are thinking clearly. Not even me."

Kiera agreed on that point.

She didn't stop him as he walked away with Meiying in tow. The final straw that had broken their bonds of friendship hadn't been a serial killer, monstrous fairies, or terrifying gargoyles. It had been their own obsessions.

Kiera desperately hoped Ben's paranoia was wrong. She was tired of constantly looking over her shoulder and being unable to trust magic. She wanted to believe that the strange spirit lingering beside her and silently urging her to follow that tug downwards was good. She was tired of being attacked and hunted. For once, she wanted things to be nice and safe. Believing Ben would get rid of that security she was trying to build around herself.

So she chose to keep going to class, even though the flame of suspicious had been lit once again for what felt like the tenth time.

Tucker got up from the table too, taking his tray and apple core with him as he walked away. He didn't even say goodbye. They were all beaten down by this point. Greetings and farewells wouldn't change that right now.

11

The next lesson with Kent offered a nice respite from the depressed, lonely life Kiera was beginning to live. The feeling of exhilaration from having her memories returned as soon as she walked through the door brought a bit of life back into her. Then, when Kent said she'd be the first to enter the spirit world today, it became the cherry on top. Entering the spirit realm meant another chance, albeit a brief one, to investigate the figures down there who were beginning to follow her around in real life. It also gave her a chance to follow that tug and decide whether Kent was a kind guide or a shrewd manipulator. Her mind liked the former characterization, but her gut told her the latter. Kent's smile brought warmth and comfort, but sometimes she could see the cracks forming behind it.

"How long will I stay in the realm today?" she asked as Kent gestured for her to begin the spell she only knew inside this classroom.

"One minute in the real world, so an hour in theirs." He paused, as though he'd just said something he shouldn't have. "In the spirit realm, that is," he said, then waved his hand again, forcing her to get on with it. "We only have twenty minutes before the rest of the lesson starts so I don't want to waste any more time."

She nodded, then spoke the spell without hesitation. If she practiced this spell any more times, she was sure her body would be able to speak it from muscle memory, even if Kent erased their memories. Then she could enter on her own without a time limit. The only thing that would hold her back then was her fear of the unknown dangers it could present. Kent always warned them never to go in alone, but she wasn't even sure if he was telling the truth or if he just wanted to limit them like he did with their memories.

The slip through the floor felt like second nature. She was back in the spirit realm, adjacent to reality and surrounded by the souls of her spirits. They looked darker than before. The pinks had turned red, the sky blue to navy, and the lime greens into forest greens. Kiera was curious how hers looked too.

The spirit that had latched onto her a month ago was still by her side, just as featureless and silent as ever. She was so used to it by now that she didn't even acknowledge it. What she *did* acknowledge this time was the strange couple behind her.

About a week ago, she decided to finally face her fears and turned around to see the thing that had whispered in her ears for weeks on end. What she found had been surprising. It was two tall creatures, one clearly female and one male. The female one was the only one who spoke but her voice she used when Kiera faced her became smooth and feminine, rather than snakelike the way it had been when her back had been turned. The lady didn't utter anymore threats. She simply implored Kiera to join her, to use her magic, and to come closer. Kiera only followed one of those orders, the use of magic one, but it wasn't because the lady told her to.

"Don't follow me," Kiera instructed the couple, unsure if they'd obey but hoping they would. Today, she was determined to follow the tug and find what it led to. The first time she had followed it, she had finally encountered the spirit lingering next to her now. Hopefully the next time she found the source, she'd discover this spirit's true body or motivation or at least *something*. Anything was better than being stopped by the hard ground in real life, preventing her from going deeper. Only in the spirit world were the walls and barriers gone.

She marched forward, sometimes feeling like her body really existed and sometimes not. The spirit following along beside her, the kind one, seemed eager for her to proceed.

But then something slipped into her way, blocking the light in front of her. It was tall and had long hair, but Kiera could tell by its shadow that it had the build of a man. It was the male half of the pair... and was that a sword he had in his hand? Or had he just turned his own hand into a blade? She couldn't tell.

Fear struck her and she took a step back, only to bump into the figure of the woman behind her. The female leaned down as soon as Kiera moved away, her breath cold on the side of Kiera's face.

"Fine," the woman told her, sounding like a disgruntled mother dealing with an immature daughter. "It's clear you don't plan to join me without receiving something in return. I can respect a woman who knows how to negotiate."

The straightforward manner of her voice felt so

different from her usual, raspy and almost ancient accent that it gave Kiera a start. It felt like the woman was doing a poor imitation of the modern-day dialect.

"I will answer all your questions as long as you stay here with me," the woman finished, sending shivers up Kiera's spine, or whatever substitute she had for a spine now.

The spirit next to Kiera seemed restless and anxious. Something about the way it moved around her just gave her the feeling that it wanted to grab her by the arm and pull her away but couldn't.

Everything in Kiera's body told her to run away from this couple. They couldn't have good intentions. It felt like they were just trying to stall her. She should just tell them no and keep going—

No. That wouldn't be smart.

"Fine," Kiera said, doing her best to raise her chin. "Go ahead. Tell me everything."

The woman paused, then sighed. "I cannot answer questions if you have not given them first," she said, reminding Kiera of Kent for some reason. That was odd, since Kiera couldn't recall a time Kent had ever outright acted tired of her. It still felt so familiar, though, like maybe he had in another life.

Kiera stepped back, trying to veer away from

the man blocking her path so she could get past him. She could hear heavy breathing coming from him now, like he was in pain. Why didn't he speak? Was he just a servant to the woman?

"Kiera," the woman called as Kiera continued backing up. She was right in line with the male now and could make a dash for it, but there was no guarantee she could get away. "Kiera, why are you running from me?"

Kiera glanced at the woman's shadow, then froze when she felt more than saw the male thing move. He was right behind her again, blocking her way. There'd be no getting around him. He was too fast.

That meant she had to fight.

She felt her magic return to her, feeling stronger and more present down here than before. It felt excited too, like puppies about to play in a park. It was ready to join her in battle against this weird, unnamed couple.

"Just grab her, Kilon," the woman said suddenly. Kilon? The god of law? Something about the way the woman said it was odd too. It felt like she was acting, like she didn't actually want this Kilon man to grab Kiera. Was she bluffing? Why?

It didn't matter. Regardless, Kiera already had a death spell planned. If that didn't work, now would be a good time to see how the elements acted down here.

Keeping track of where both the man and woman were, Kiera leapt backwards away from both of them, then finally uttered the words for a death spell, aiming it at the man. As soon as she started whispering the chant, he raised his hand, which was indeed a sword embedded into his skin. He then darted toward her, so fast she could barely register him.

The final word uttered, her magic leapt into action, moving toward the man just as fast as it moved toward him. The two clashed in the middle, with him swinging his blade right at the spell. The sword felt so unnatural and wrong that Kiera was sure she'd seen this man before, but looking a little different. There were so many memories that felt right on the edge of her mind, unable to accessed.

All worries about memory loss vanished as soon as the blade touched where she knew the magic was. There was a small flash of light at the impact, revealing the scarred face and tied-up mouth of Kilon, then she felt her own magic simply... vanish.

Her knees went weak as she felt a fifth of her magic just up and disappear. No, wait. It didn't disappear. She gasped as Kilon raised his blade and the magic began to swirl around it. It hadn't vanished. He had *taken* it from her somehow and was using it as his own. The magic that he hadn't managed to touch with his sword raced back to Kiera but she still felt weaker.

Beside her, the woman laughed. "Excellent, Kilon! This is why we keep you around, little Kiera. Your magic is so much stronger when you've played with it for a while. Use it on me next time. I've so longed to have magic of my own again."

"What?" Kiera backed away from both of them, feeling like a sheep cornered by two very hungry wolves. She couldn't use her magic on these two. Spells only strengthened them somehow, letting them steal from her. Were they using a spell she didn't know? Or...

Now things made sense. If that man was Kilon, this woman was Vara, the goddess of death. Of course she knew things Kiera didn't.

The tug felt even stronger now, insistent and desperate. She had to get to it before these two drained her of every bit of magic. Then, when she had run out, she was sure they'd steal her very life away too.

Kilon and Vara stepped toward her. Vara giggled maniacally. They thought they'd won.

With nowhere else to go, Kiera gave up on the wish to have a real body in here and allowed herself to shoot straight down. She'd been held back by the notion that one needed to walk straight in this place. She had treated it like Earth, with gravity and solid ground, but that wasn't how things worked down here. The tug was below and behind her, so that's how she had to move now, down and backwards.

As she ran, she cast a speed spell on herself. From what she saw, she assumed the pair could only steal her magic if they got their hands on it. If she used spells only on herself, they hopefully wouldn't be able to do anything.

The tug led her forward, getting closer and closer until she could see a third figure in the distance. It couldn't be Kilon, since the god of Rule and Laws was currently chasing after her. Plus, this new figure was shorter, a more normal height for a real human.

The spirit who had been by her side all this time rushed ahead of her, toward the figure.

Kiera heard a grunt, more akin to a bear than a man, and felt Kilon's other hand grasp her shoulder. He was trying to stop her. She couldn't let him!

She felt a bit of magic leave her when he grabbed her, ruining her previous theory. He was still taking the magic from her with a mere touch. The only advantage from that was that the new magic gained seemed to stop him in his tracks for a moment, like a hound being halted in a chase because he found meat placed on the road before him. The magic was a distraction, bait. It gave Kiera the last second that she needed to reach the true origin of the pull that had been tugging on her for over a month.

"Kiera?" the new voice said, young and male. He sounded so familiar and... comfortable. A blast of warm, wonderful heat shot through her heart.

The figure turned toward her just as she ran into him, bumping against his chest, though without a human form, it wasn't painful or loud.

As soon as she touched the person, the shadow around him vanished and she could make out his face clearly. He was handsome, around her age, and with the gaunt cheeks of a sick person. His skin was pale too, with a few cuts around his eyes that looked fresh.

It was Ezra.

As soon as she touched him and the spirit beside her leapt into this body, she immediately knew who Ezra was. All the memories came rushing back, of him, of Kent, of Vara and Kilon, and of what Kent had done to her the day before Christmas break began. Kent had kidnapped Ezra somehow and then wiped her memories of him so Kiera wouldn't try to stop him.

She remembered everything.

"Come find me," Ezra whispered, his eyes wide with fear. "Kiera—" He seemed ready to say something else, but then a new hand grabbed the back of Kiera's shoulder and yanked her backwards. At first, she feared it was Kilon but then she felt herself falling through the floor and knew it must be Kent. He was bringing her back to the real world, away from Ezra.

She reached for Ezra as she went, hoping he knew she'd try to find him. He was alive and needed help!

She wouldn't forget him again!

12

Kent was studying Kiera intently as she settled back into her chair, her mind racing from everything that had just happened. He stayed quiet as he removed his hand from her shoulder and walked back to his seat, though his gaze never left her face. Her emotions must be written all over it. All the other students were staring at her, some of them looking frightened by her wide eyes and heavy breathing—the new ones in particular still weren't sure how they felt about the spirit realm—but others were used to such reactions by this point and looked eager to go on their own journey into the realm instead.

"Did you experience anything different?" Kent finally prodded, his words slow and careful. "Did you learn anything new?"

He was trying to figure out if she'd discovered Ezra or her memories had returned. If that happened, he'd be sure to erase them again, just like he had two other times. She had to ensure that never happened again. She had to pretend everything had gone just as he wanted.

"I feel a little weaker," she admitted, using the truth to disguise Ezra's presence. She'd bring up the goddess instead to distract Kent. "I saw two figures in there. One was a man and one was a woman."

"Oh?" Kent leaned back in his chair, already comfortable with the prospect. "Did they say anything to you?"

"Just that they wanted me to join them," Kiera said. "Do you know who they are?" Hopefully her acting was good enough to deceive him. She didn't sense him using any truth spells on her but he was a higher-level magician. He might be able to disguise such a thing. She hated how little she knew about him and his magic skills.

"No, I don't," he lied, looking satisfied. "Anything else? You mentioned feeling weaker."

"Yes, just tired, like I ran a marathon." Shoot. Hopefully that wouldn't hint at her run toward Ezra. "I feel like my magic is weaker."

"Interesting." He looked genuinely curious.

"Very few people have such a firm grasp on magic and its presence. Keep an eye on this and let me know if your magic feels weaker again. We wouldn't want you losing your connection or anything."

Kiera was sure that was precisely what he wanted. He kept sending her in there so the goddess Vara could steal her magic. She remembered all his schemes now. He was probably stealing from the other students too, though it was so gradual that they wouldn't notice. That might explain why Ezra had become so gaunt and weak last semester.

She was so glad her memories were back. Everything was falling into place now that she didn't have someone in the back of her head, stealing everything important.

Continuing her charade as a tired student, she listened dutifully to Kent's lecture as she normally did and watched as the other students entered the spirit realm, which mainly consisted of their body freezing up while they went in. It was like going to sleep with your eyes open and it only lasted a minute or two before they returned. Kent would stay by their side, uttering spells as they did so, protecting them in case of an emergency. Kiera was glad he couldn't see into the realm during that time, at least judging by his reaction to her lies. He seemed oblivious to her discovery of Ezra.

Speaking of Ezra, now that her memories had returned, she could remember why that persistent tug had come to exist in the first place. It wasn't the power of love pulling her toward Ezra or anything. She had negotiated with Vara, right before her memory wipe, and the goddess had agreed to give her a power that would help her lost lover. The tug must have been that power. But the goddess played dirty. She gave Kiera the power but told Kent to erase her memory so Kiera couldn't use the power effectively.

Kiera wasn't sure why encountering Ezra again had released the spell. Maybe there had been a loophole weaved into the spell, something like encountering the person himself would bring the memories back, and that was how it broke.

There were a lot of things she couldn't quite wrap her head around yet, but what mattered was that she now knew about Ezra again and could finally launch a proper rescue mission. She could still feel Ezra pulling on her, even in the real world, which meant he was still here somewhere... If the tug was leading down, even on Earth and outside the spirit world, then he must be underground. How could that be?

She thought back on what happened in the spirit world, trying to recall anything she'd missed up front. She'd been so focused on Ezra but there had been other things around him now that she thought about it. First of all, he still looked sickly and had a few cuts. That meant he was still being drained, so Kent must be the one who had him if Kent really was working with Vara and Kilon.

As soon as she touched Ezra, she'd felt a few other presences too, people around him. He wasn't alone. Maybe it was the other students who had left the class. Kent had claimed some students quit over the holidays, but what if they'd been kidnapped too?

Dang it! She wished she'd paid more attention to his surroundings. That could have given a clue as to where he was and who specifically he was with. Now her only option might be going back into the spirit realm, which she now knew had two old gods waiting to slowly sip away all her magic. Was it worth losing her magic in order to find Ezra?

What a stupid question. Of course it was worth it. She loved Ezra and no amount of magic was more important than keeping him alive.

Kiera kept her expression neutral as the class wrapped up and felt Kent's eyes on her multiple times throughout. She hoped she didn't look too normal. That would give it away just as easily as acting strange.

"Class dismissed," Kent said, still focusing on Kiera as she packed up her things. "And Kiera?"

"Yes?" She looked up at him and tried to mask her fear of him.

"Please let me know if you encounter anything strange when you're down there, okay?" he repeated, making her bristle. "I would hate to see you get hurt."

"Thanks," she said as naturally as she could. "I'll be sure to let you know."

She only allowed herself to breathe a sigh of relief once the door had closed behind her and she was free. Strangely, even as she stepped through the doorway, she didn't feel her memories disappear as she left, even though the ones of how to enter the spirit realm did. The classroom memory loss spell still had power over her, but Kent's other spell stealing Ezra from her did not. That was good to know. Sadly, that meant she could still only enter the spirit realm in Kent's classes, but at least she could investigate everything else without him peering over her shoulder.

It was time to confront Tucker about this and ask for his help... as well as admit to Ben that he was right all along. She'd have a lot of apologies to give to him and he'd probably demand something like groveling to make up for it. She wasn't looking forward to that.

13

Even though Ezra's pull wasn't physically stronger than it was before, it certainly felt like it as Kiera exited the bowels of the necromancy building and followed the path toward the dorms. She planned to drop off her books and backpack, then meet up with Tucker and Ben in the cafeteria so they could discuss what to do next. She figured Sally and Meiying could help too, if they wanted. They were part of the group now, even though they hadn't been as close to Ezra as she and Tucker were.

Every second wasted felt like it was bringing Ezra closer to death. His skin had looked so grey, his eyes so big against his sunken face and tight skin, that Kiera had genuinely feared he might collapse then and there. He'd been locked up wherever he was for over a month and Kiera doubted Kent treated him and the other captives well.

It was clear Kent had viewed Ezra as a rival from the beginning, even if all Ezra ever wanted was a kind elder brother to look up to. Once Kent was caught using necromancy for evil things and Ezra was named the next necromancer in the family, set to inherit all the roles Kent would have had, Kiera was sure Kent came to resent his youngest sibling. There was little familial, brotherly love in their relationship. In Kent's eyes, Ezra was just a pawn and a challenge to overcome. He probably planned to kill Ezra once he'd drained as much magic and life from him as he could.

Kiera could already picture Kent literally sacrificing Ezra and the other students to the goddess Vara as a sacrifice. What had she offered Kent in return? Power? Immortality? Maybe both. Kiera hated to imagine an evil man like Kent living forever.

One thing Kiera realized as she ascended the dorm elevator, then dropped off her backpack inside her room, was that the spirit she now knew had belonged to Ezra was gone. It had been reunited with his body so there was no need to follow her anymore... probably. She still wasn't sure how that worked. Maybe Ezra was using magic on his end and it had its own strange limits, or maybe the magic was just working on its own, trying to bring them together to stop the goddess. She might never know the answer to that.

All she knew was the intense loneliness Ezra's absence had brought yet again. She almost missed having her memories stolen from her. At least then she had nothing to miss. IgKierance had been bliss. Now she truly felt empty again without him by her side. The only positive her memories brought was an intense drive to bring Ezra back and rid herself of feeling cut in two. She had to get her other half back.

That passion burned in her as she went back outside, then into the cafeteria to hunt down her friends. It was time to enlist them for a mission, maybe their final one if she ended up leaving the university once the semester was done... or if they wound up dead. Either way, this would be their final quest together. Best to make it count.

Kiera immediately spotted Tucker and Sally sitting with four other students at one of the corner tables. Tucker was laughing along with one of the other boys and Sally was chatting with one of the girls. They were both the type to blend into groups really easily, with their natural charm and outgoing personalities.

Meanwhile, Ben and Meiying were seated at one of the corner tables with some of Ben's gamer friends. Meiying was reading a book while Ben spoke with his buddies, his expression grim. Kiera could immediately tell he still wasn't over their past argument. At least Meiying was still by his side. Kiera would have hated to see her best friend become completely isolated.

Their friend group had split into two.

Now, which person should she go to first? Kiera knew talking to Tucker would be easier. He wasn't the type to hold a grudge like Ben. But she also knew doing that would make convincing Ben to join even harder, since they both knew Kiera should go to Ben first. They were childhood friends, after all. They'd been through fights like this before, so Kiera knew Ben would get over their past arguments eventually, but she didn't have the time to sit through his sulking or resistance. Time was not on their side. She needed to apologize quickly and get him on board as fast as she could.

So, after taking less than a second to think about it, Kiera didn't bother grabbing any food and made a beeline straight for Ben's table. As soon as their eyes met, he looked both elated that she had come to apologize and also nervous about the coming conversation. That dread would probably leave once she told him what she'd discovered about Ezra. Plus, he'd get to say he told her so.

"Hey, Ben," Kiera said, feeling more than just Ben and Meiying's eyes swing toward her as she stopped in front of the table. "How's it going?" She kept her tone of voice slightly off, higher than usual, to tip him off that they should be on guard. Kent might be listening in.

Luckily, the flicker in his eyes told her he caught her meaning immediately. They knew each other best after all.

But that didn't stop him from continuing to act pissed at her. "Welcome back, Kiera. Come to apologize?" he asked, keeping his voice loud enough so his friends stopped what they were doing and started listening. An awkward silence covered the table, as well as a few other ones nearby. Kiera was sure Tucker and Sally had started listening in from across the room too.

"I just wanted to say," Kiera said slowly, keeping her words slow and precise. Kent might be using some form of magic to eavesdrop. She couldn't show her cards just yet, especially with other students nearby. "I just wanted to say that you were right."

Ben's frown faltered slightly, not just because Kiera apologized but because of the implications of her words. If he was right, that meant Kent really was a villain interfering with their lives. This also meant Kiera had learned something new that she couldn't say out loud.

"Right," he said quietly, then cleared his throat. "If you came here to grovel, go ahead. You guys can leave," he said to the other guys at the table, excluding Meiying. The boys looked eager to escape the awkward conversation. As they grabbed their food trays and left, Tucker and Sally walked up behind Kiera to join in.

"She said I was right," Ben said to Tucker immediately. Tucker had opened his mouth to say something but shut it as soon as Ben said that. Now all three of them—Kiera, Ben, and Tucker—knew what the situation was and how serious things had become. They had to figure out how to discuss Kiera's new discovery without being overheard by Kent. That would be hard, since magic was detectable, especially by high level magicians, so even if they cast a spell to keep their conversation private, Kent would know they used magic and be suspicious. This made talking difficult.

"Don't sit down," Ben said before Tucker and Kiera could do just that. "Let's discuss this outside. I'm done eating anyway. Wouldn't want the whole school to know about our fight, right?"

Kiera rolled her eyes for show. He didn't actually care if the students heard them fight. What he did care about was revealing their knowledge to Kent.

In two minutes, they had disposed of their food trays and were outside, heading toward the garden at the back of the university grounds. It would offer some privacy, since no one wanted to go there in the middle of winter, but it wouldn't leave them as vulnerable to attack either. There were some security guards nearby who could protect them if any fairies or gargoyles showed up.

"So," Ben said as they all stopped in the middle of the garden, surrounded by green and purple trees that still had leaves despite the cold weather. Some flowers were wilting slightly, which meant the magician in charge of gardening was slacking off... or Kent was having some effect on the grounds. Kiera wasn't sure she wanted to believe the second one, since the implications of that meant things had gotten pretty bad.

Tucker held up his hand to prevent Ben from speaking. There could be spies everywhere.

Kiera was biting her lip, trying to think of a solution to their problem, when Ben suddenly started chanting some magical words.

"Wait, Ben," Kiera hissed, worried they might

give themselves away. But then Ben shook his head at her, acting so confident that she had to believe he knew what he was doing. Despite his attitude, he was still one of the best magicians among them, after all.

After finishing the chant, Kiera watched as what looked like a blurry bubble surrounded them. Her breathing felt hollow too, like there was no air around them.

"We'll sound funny when we talk," Ben explained, his voice higher than normal. "But no one can hear us, even with a magical spell."

"But if Kent was spying on us," Tucker countered. "He would have heard you utter the spell."

"I cast *another* spell before that to silence my voice to everyone but us, then used a memory erasure spell in the surrounding area beforehand too," Ben said, puffing up his chest.

"I hate to break it to you," Sally said, "but if someone like Professor Kent is watching, won't he get suspicious that we're all suddenly silent or gone or whatever this spell does?"

"Nope. I prepared for that too. I cast a *fourth* spell that would make it sound like we're arguing right now. If he listens in, he'll just hear me and Kiera arguing about my mismatching socks and the comic books I stole from her three years ago."

"That was you?" Kiera muttered. "But there's one more thing. He'll know we've just used magic and will immediately start to investigate."

"Way ahead of you," Ben said, beginning to impress even Kiera by this point. "Since I always knew we might need to face up against the guy someday, I started studying like crazy to master high level spells." He flashed all of them a proud grin. "Meiying and I have mastered some spells that not even our teachers can do."

"That's... very impressive." Kiera was genuinely shocked. "I can't believe it."

"You can't believe that I managed to study?" Ben finished for her.

"Yes." Kiera suppressed a laugh, then frowned at the strange walls surrounding them. "How long do we have?"

"As long as we need. I prepared a whole hour of fighting."

Tucker chuckled and glanced at Kiera. "How often do you two fight?"

"Enough," Ben answered. "The point is, I'm ready for whatever Kent throws at us. Whatever it is he's up to, I want to get rid of it so this annoying hole in my memory can come back. Plus, I want to rub that smug grin off his face."

"If you were able to use high level spells so

easily, why didn't you teach them to the rest of us?" Tucker asked, to which Ben shrugged.

"Who said it was easy?"

"Okay." Kiera raised her voice to bring their attention back to the present. "We need to focus. I don't want Kent to get suspicious so I'll explain everything as fast as I can."

"And with detail," Tucker added, not one to skip over things. He and Ben felt like polar opposites at times.

"And with detail." Kiera took a deep breath, remembering that Kent had wiped all their memories and maybe everyone in the entire school, excluding people who were powerful enough to prevent it like the headmaster. She'd have to fill in a ton of gaps Ezra's presence had left and explain it all in a few minutes. "Okay. Here goes."

14

Everyone listened in complete silence as Kiera recounted what she'd discovered and guessed what type of memories all of them had lost. Most of it related to Ezra, with only a few memories of Kent being a jerk also being deleted. The only movement any of them made was Ben occasionally pumping his fist into the air, elated that some of his guesses had been right.

"So," Tucker said once all was said and done. "What's our next step? You said there are other students trapped as well so there must be some parents already raising an alarm. We should tell the headmaster what happened."

"I'm not sure about that." Sally raised a hand to stop him. "If what Kiera said about your last encounter with him is true, the headmaster already knows the general stuff. We'd just be confirming what he already suspects. We wouldn't have new information to give him, unless Kiera finds some way to remember how to enter the spirit realm outside the classroom."

"But we need help," Ben whined, a month's worth of waiting wearing him down.

"Without evidence, there's not much we can do," Sally said. "All we know is some people are missing and they're still alive. The headmaster already suspects that. We could warn him, sure, but that would tip off Kent and we might lose all our memories again."

"So we write something down," Ben countered. "He can't erase items too, can he?"

Kiera looked to the others, unsure how to answer that. Then she said, "Now that I think about it, I think he might be able to. When you and I found a photo of Ezra and I together, I kept it with me. Then, when our memories were erased again, I don't recall ever finding it."

"Great!" Ben threw his hands in the air in annoyance. Meanwhile, Meiying leaned toward Kiera.

"Ezra kept a picture of you? That's cute," she said, smiling sweetly.

"Your boyfriend doesn't keep any photos of you?" Sally asked sarcastically, ignoring Ben as she talked about him. "That's pathetic."

"As much as I enjoy making fun of Ben," Tucker cut in, "we need to be serious about this. We need to find Ezra and potentially tell his uncle about him, without alerting one of the most powerful magicians on campus. I need more ideas on what to do."

"Well, I can follow the pull the goddess gave me," Kiera suggested. "But it seems to lead underground."

"But you could access him inside the spirit world," Ben said. "Is there some way to move your physical body to that location via the spirit realm?"

"I don't know. I don't think so. I always return to my chair, regardless of how far I've moved in the realm."

"So either there's more to the spirit realm than you've been taught or there's a physical entrance underground," Meiying said, frowning as she thought about it. "So we should keep an eye out for any secret doors or wells that might lead us there."

"Wells?" Ben asked. "Here?"

Meiying shrugged, looking as baffled as the rest of them.

Ben looked ready to speak again when he

suddenly tilted his head, listening to something else. His eyes widened. "Kent's on his way. I'm sending us all back into the normal world. Kiera, you and me need to be fighting right away. Meiying, try to calm me down. Tucker look upset. Sally, just enjoy the fight, I guess."

"Is this an indication of how you view us?" Tucker muttered as Ben started whispering the words that would break his spell. Then he began to count down.

"Three. Two. One. Maybe if you got a boyfriend, Kiera, we wouldn't have to constantly listen to you whine about being so lonely!"

Kiera was almost caught off guard by both the bubble vanishing, returning them to the normal garden and sounds without an empty echo, and also Ben's sudden shift from quiet counting to outright shouting. He must know where the conversation was and slipped in so the illusion wouldn't break.

She had to gulp, giving herself a second to think of a comeback and look furious at the same time. Then she shouted an insult back at him as the others got into character. "That's rich, coming from a guy who *does* have a girlfriend yet still manages to whine about everything around him!"

"Guys, just stop," Meiying said, perfectly slipping into her role of concerned girlfriend by trying to step between them. Unfortunately for her, Kiera and Ben knew how to fight without looking at each other. They used to argue on the phone or through a headset while playing games together.

"Sounds like you're afraid to admit that you're too stubborn to admit when you're wrong. No man would want to put up with someone as hardheaded as you!" Ben countered, ignoring Meiying as she tried to push him away. He was bigger than her and, while he normally would have caved to Meiying, his pretend anger prevented it this time around.

Kiera opened her mouth, preparing an equally angry tirade on the spot, when Kent stepped into view and interrupted. He had an amused smirk on his face, but it was wiped away pretty easily and replaced by the façade of a teacher worried about his students.

"Ben, Kiera, please," he said, holding up his hands like a religious figure coming to bring peace. "I've received complaints about your argument. If you're going to fight, especially for this long, at least do it in a place of relative privacy."

"Like I'd want to be alone with someone like her," Ben sneered, jerking his head toward Kiera as though he hated the sight of her. "I was done with the conversation anyway."

"Same here," Kiera replied, keeping her voice

low like she was both pissed off and embarrassed. "You can rest assured I won't be apologizing to you again, Benjamin."

"Likewise. Let's go, Meiying." Ben then wrapped an arm around his girlfriend's shoulders and led her away, escaping Kent. Kiera felt jealous. She didn't want to talk to the teacher now that her hatred for him had returned, especially if Kent had just heard a heated argument she hadn't been present for. He might ask her about something her illusion-self said and she wouldn't know how to answer.

"Is there anything I can do to help?" Kent asked, turning back to Kiera. His fake attempts to help them felt even more grating than before. Nothing was worse than having a man smile at you while he held your lover captive.

"No," Kiera said, huffing as though Ben had just called her the worst name in existence. "Sorry you had to hear that. It's just... when Ben and I fight, we have a lot of ammo from past fights to bring up. It's just personal gripes, that's all."

Please buy the lie. Please buy the lie.

"I'll make sure things don't get physical," Tucker added when Kent didn't say anything.

"What were you two arguing about?" Kent asked and Kiera forced herself to not freeze up.

Ben hadn't exactly told them what the topic was. Did he actually make them fight about his suspicions about Kent? Or was it just a fight about Ben stealing one of her books again or something? He shouldn't have walked away like that, the idiot. He was so smart at times, yet all logic went out the window when he wanted to procrastinate or avoid situations like this.

"It's... personal," Kiera said finally, forcing as much genuine pain into her voice as possible. "I'd rather not talk about it, no offense."

"None taken," Kent said, though Kiera could feel him looking her up and down. Best to stay silent for now. Kent had heard their fight, or at least some of it, so if she gave an actual answer and was wrong, he'd know something was up.

"Just..." Kent chuckled. "Try to keep your fights private or at least keep your voices low from now on. It's rude to do stuff like this and inconvenience others."

"I know. I'm sorry." Kiera bowed her head, growing tired of acting.

"Then I'll see you in class." She heard Kent walk away, then glanced at Tucker and Sally, who were watching him leave. They couldn't speak about any of this again, lest Kent hear them. They'd have to either speak in code from now on or wait for Ben to use another high-level spell. Maybe Tucker could learn some of those spells too. That way if something happened to Ben and Meiying, they'd have some backup.

"It's getting dark," Tucker commented, glancing at their surroundings, especially at the outskirts of the woods. "Tomorrow, I'm gonna go for a walk around the grounds. Sally, do you want to come?"

Aka, he planned to look around for that underground entrance.

"Sure," Sally said, smiling at him and then nodding at Kiera. "Good luck during your special classes." She was hinting at Kiera trying to find the entrance in the spirit realm during class, or at least some clue toward where Ezra might be.

"Thanks." Kiera nodded back at her, then dreaded going to sleep tonight. It would be hard to calm down enough to rest now that her head was filled with nothing but Ezra being tortured underneath their very feet while they did nothing.

"I think I'm going to speak to some relatives of mine too," Tucker added quietly as they prepared to head back to the dorms. "Update them on how my grades are going."

They were good at speaking in code, Kiera

noted. He probably meant he would get word of this to the headmaster somehow, hopefully without letting Kent know it was happening. This felt like a spy mission, which normally would have excited Kiera if she wasn't so worried about Ezra.

"Just be careful not to piss them off when they find out about your low marks on that one test," Kiera told him, trying to use "codes" as well. "They'll kill you if they find out you came close to failing."

"Right." Tucker gave a fake but perfect laugh. "I know." If they got caught, their memories might not be the only thing at stake. Kent might get fed up and kill Ezra outright just to get them off his back. What was worse, Kiera might never know Ezra was dead until months in the future. She might risk the lives of everyone around her, only to find a corpse at the end of the journey. The thought terrified her.

"See you guys tomorrow," Sally said, patting Kiera on the back for comfort. "I'll meet you at breakfast."

This wasn't the first time Kiera had come to appreciate having so many friends. Not only did she have Ben for most of her life, who could read her like a book and would overcome any argument to protect her, but she also had three other loyal friends now too who were ready to look out for. Now there was only one person missing from their crew who tied them all together. Ezra. Kiera prayed he could hold out until they found him.

15

The days that followed their discovery of Ezra's existence were tough. Kiera now had to attend classes and sit a few rows away from the man she knew had stolen her lover. She was forced to smile and answer politely when Kent asked her a question, all the while afraid that he would discovery her and erase her memories yet again. If word of Sally's message to the headmaster got to Kent, he might do it then too, or maybe even launch an attack on them and kill them. Kiera wouldn't be surprised if another gargoyle snuck up on her and crushed her in her sleep. The only thing holding Kent back from killing her right now, as far as she could tell, was her connection to magic. He often commented on it and the goddess Vara had as well. That might be the only thing keeping her alive and, in turn, Ezra. They couldn't risk losing such powerful pawns.

Halfway through the week, after her classes had ended, Kiera headed toward the gardens rather than into the cafeteria. She wasn't hungry today. Her stomach was in knots from trying to cast a particularly difficult teleportation spell and failing. If the teacher, a kind woman with eyes like a hawk, hadn't realized her mistake, Kiera might have accidentally cut her own body in two. Now she was on edge and didn't feel like chatting with her friends, all the while being unable to talk about Ezra.

She kept her head down as she passed people on the path, letting her dark hair fall over her eyes. A few people glanced at her as she passed. She wasn't the most popular student here but she was well-known for fighting off several monsters by this point. It was hard to blend in like she used to.

When she reached the garden, a separate space shielded by beautiful trees of many colors, she noticed someone sitting on one of the benches inside. People normally weren't in the gardens around this time, since the cafeteria was only open for two hours per meal, so most people crowded in to get food while they could. Who else was sitting in the garden? He was too cloaked in the shadow of the trees to be recognizable.

The man was slouched over in the seat, his elbows resting on his knees and head turned down. His dark hair and skin, along with his strong build, made Kiera assume it might be Tucker. Sure enough, when she stepped on a branch and it snapped, he looked up to see who was approaching. It was Tucker and he didn't look well. His eyes were sunken into his face, his mouth was turned downwards in a sullen frown, and his eyes were dark, like he'd been thinking cruel thoughts, which wasn't like him. Tucker was serious and studious but never aggressive or violent.

"Are you okay?" Kiera asked cautiously as she approached, thinking of things like possession and alternate personalities as she got closer. She wouldn't be surprised if Kent possessed Tucker and made him kill her, then framed Tucker for the murder. But that worry vanished when Tucker shook his head and leaned back in the bench, his normal expression returning.

"I'm just thinking about... him... and how he's really gone," Tucker said sadly, each word slow and well thought out. He must be referring to Ezra while trying not to let any eavesdroppers realize it.

Kiera nodded. "Your father, right?" she lied, catching his drift and letting him know she knew the real topic of discussion.

"Right." Tucker looked down again, sighing. "I just... wish I'd been there for him while he was still with us. We were always so close and... I failed him."

Pity swept through Kiera. Tucker and Ezra were best friends for years. Out of the entire group, he'd been the closest to him. She was sure Tucker felt the same guilt she had for forgetting Ezra. It wasn't their fault, but it felt like they should have at least noticed his absence, even without their memories of him. It was like having someone die and realizing you've forgotten about them after a while.

"It wasn't your fault," she told him quietly, taking a seat beside him and leaning back like he was, letting the cool air blow through her hair. "If he was still here, he'd assure you there wasn't anything you could have done."

She heard Tucker grind his teeth. "I feel so helpless, sitting here doing nothing while he wastes away."

"We're—*you're* not doing nothing," Kiera cut in. She wasn't good at giving pep talks or offering advice, so all these words felt awkward on her tongue. "You'll get him back."

Tucker scoffed, his voice filled with disgust. "Fat chance of that." He paused and glanced at her, remorseful. "Sorry. I don't want to sound harsh. I know you're just trying to be nice."

"No." Kiera allowed herself to frown this time. "I know exactly how you feel. I feel the same way." They both wanted to find and rescue Ezra right now, this very second. Waiting around could create nothing but a corpse at the end of their path, as she said before. There *had* to be something else they could do.

"Let's take a walk," she told him, getting up suddenly and focusing on the tugging feeling that never went away.

"Okay?" Tucker did so too, studying her to see what she was up to. "Where are we going?"

"Anywhere." She really hated speaking so vaguely about everything. It was becoming infuriating and only made her more mad at Kent. "I'll lead the way. Keep an eye out for anything... suspicious." She gulped, hoping she got the point across. She wanted him to scan the area for Ezra or a secret entrance or anything. "Scan the area while we go," she added when he still looked confused. "I don't want a gargoyle sneaking up on us or anything. Not again."

"Ah." He nodded and smirked, finally getting her point. They weren't just going on a walk. She was going to take him right to the source of the tug and, using the excuse that they were looking for gargoyles and other threats, she'd make him scan the ground beneath their feet to search for the source of the tug. "Lead the way, ma'am."

Kiera nodded and exited the garden, headed toward the center of the grounds where the water fountain stood. She'd been there before but hadn't been able to scan the ground yet. Ben and Tucker were better at those types of spells.

"Oh, and Kiera?" Tucker asked, stopping her in her tracks.

"What is it?"

"Thanks, for encouraging me. I'm sure he—my dad—would appreciate it."

She nodded again, allowing a genuine smile to come over her face again. It was nice to know they were all in this together and shared the same guilt over forgetting Ezra. They'd make up for it by finding him now.

The pair blended in easily this time as they walked down the path, which was less busy now that most people had headed to the cafeteria. Tucker started muttering a seeing spell, casting it about wildly to give the illusion that he really was just looking for gargoyles. Kiera noticed him looking downwards, though, and she did the same.

The tug finally led them right to the water fountain, the mist from the flying water lightly hitting them, and then Kiera stepped a few feet past it, reaching the exact spot where the tug was the strongest. She hoped Kent wouldn't find this suspicious if he was watching. If there really was something underground or Ezra was trapped in the spirit realm, then she technically wasn't in the right spot but above it. That shouldn't look suspicious, right?

Trying to feign indifference, she sat on the edge of the waterfall instead of standing in the exact spot, then glanced at Tucker. "No gargoyles?" she asked. "Or fairies?"

"Or serial killers?" he added, then waved the spell around, starting in the air before making his way down. Good. He wasn't acting suspicious.

His face remained blank during most of the spell. Only when he cast it downwards did his expression shift slightly. His flat mouth curved down and he squinted, then he swept all expressions away again.

"Nothing?" she asked, hopeful. There had to be something here. This was their only lead, other than reentering the spirit world, and she could only do that in Kent's classes.

Tucker shut his mouth, ending the spell. "No monsters," he said quietly, but he paused, looking ready to say more. Had he found something?

Dang it! She should have figured out some spell that only allowed them to speak into each other's minds... but then Kent might be able to detect that one too. This was so frustrating!

"Just a lot of people," Tucker continued finally after thinking a little bit. "And some animals in the forest over there." He gestured to the trees past the buildings. "And lots of dirt beneath us. Tons of ant tunnels." He gave her a knowing look when he said that part, then continued listing things he found that were inconsequential. "There's a mole living over there. I found a woodpecker nearby that's making a nest of some sort. A couple is resting over there on that hidden bench. I'm not sure I want to know what they're doing—"

Kiera blocked him out, focusing on that other thing he said. *Tons of ant tunnels.*

Tunnels.

Were there tunnels under these grounds? Her eyes widened slightly. Was Ezra still on Earth, trapped in tunnels right beneath their feet?

"You'll have to teach me that spell sometime," she lied, cutting Tucker off before he exposed every living thing within a mile. "Would save me a lot of trouble down the road."

"Oh, it's actually a pretty common spell," Tucker continued conversing, though their eyes were telling a different story. He was staring at her, trying to determine if she'd figured out his code.

She nodded slightly. She had. Now the question was, how did they get down there? And how did they do it without raising any alarms?

"I think I'm ready for dinner now," she said. "How about you?"

"And see Ben flirting with Meiying for an hour? I don't know," Tucker pretended to hesitate. He was good at this subtly thing.

"It's gross, right?" she laughed, hoping their conversation had seemed natural. Their memories were still intact, which meant Kent hadn't noticed them investigating, right? She prayed this peace continued as they headed for the cafeteria.

Now, the next question was, how would they communicate all of this to Ben and the others? They shouldn't use Ben's argument technique twice in a row. Kent already seemed suspicious of it.

After they figured that out, they'd need to hunt down the entrance to the tunnels. Who knew what kind of traps Kent had set up down there. He'd probably hidden the entrance too. This was going to be a lot harder than she initially predicted.

16

During the rest of that week, Kiera explored the grounds with at least one other person from the friend group, searching for a tunnel entrance. She did manage to find a few old, empty wells and trash dumps at the farther parts of the woods, but nothing ever led into a series of tunnels. Things were looking bleak when the weekend swung around and by the time Kiera finished wandering around the forest with Sally, she was feeling pretty discouraged. Even when they got a little gutsy and started using searching spells despite it potentially getting Kent's attention, they still didn't find anything.

The weather was getting warmer as Kiera and Sally wandered down a dirt path back toward the campus, shoulders drooped and eyes downcast. Kiera could feel tears prick the corners of her eyes as the thought of never seeing Ezra again struck her hard.

"Well," Sally said, speaking slowly like Tucker. She normally spoke quickly, so this was out of the ordinary for her. "I don't think we'll be able to find the... flowers... that you're looking for out here." Flowers being code for Ezra and the tunnels.

"Right." Kiera waited for her to continue, hoping Sally had some solution in mind.

"We've searched the grounds high and low... but have we considered looking inside the buildings?" Sally asked quietly.

"The buildings?"

"Right. There are plenty of flower pots inside and some people like to store flowers and other plants in their basements," Sally continued, raising an eyebrow to imply they weren't discussing plants at all. "Some varieties of plant thrive in cold, dark spaces, especially of the magic variety."

"You make a good point. Which buildings do you think would house such... greenery?" Kiera asked, faltering slightly in the face of Sally's stellar acting.

"Probably the older ones, since they're more

likely to have natural, earthy basements. However, the renovations make it hard to tell which is which." Sally placed a finger under her chin, thinking, then snapped that finger against her thumb and pointed at the library. "Let's head over there for a bit. There's a book I want to show you."

Sally was so quick that Kiera had to hurry to keep up, both on her feet and in her head. She wasn't sure what Sally had planned.

The library was starting to fill up with students trickling out of the cafeteria but there was still plenty of room to head past the lobby and into the rows of endless shelves. Sally seemed to generally know where she was going, reading the alphabetical listings on the sides of the shelves before turning down a few rows. Halfway through her search, she grabbed one book off the shelf and handed it to Kiera. "Look at that while you follow me."

Kiera looked down at the book, then gasped. It was a newer book with a deep red cover and a scantily clad woman resting in the arms of tall centaur. It didn't look like the sort of reading that should be available in a school, but this was a university so most students here were at least eighteen.

"Why did you give me this?" Kiera hissed,

embarrassed to even be holding it, let alone looking at it.

Sally simply gave her a look, making Kiera pretty sure it was meant to throw anyone nearby off their trail. They weren't really here to look at harlequin novels. Sally was on the hunt for something different. Sure enough, a minute and two rows later, she found it.

"Here it is," Sally said, pulling a thin but wide book off the shelf and immediately pouring over its pages. Kiera had to peer over her shoulder to see. It was a book of blueprints. The pages started off browning and old, then transitioned into newer white papers before being replaced yet again by blueprints. The name at the top of each header said "Dreadmore Academy", though some of the earlier pages used different, older names for what the campus used to be. Sally was studying the older pages most intently. She must be searching for any mention of tunnels or at least basements built into certain buildings.

Kiera glanced over their shoulder as Sally hummed, probably blocking out her thoughts for anyone listening—if listening to one's thoughts was possible. Kiera wouldn't put it past Kent to do such a thing.

Sally was still searching the book five minutes

later, with no success, when a hush suddenly fell over the library. It made Kiera freeze up, clutching the inappropriate novel to her chest. She stared down the aisle toward the lobby, where people should be chatting and whispering as they normally did. Had something happened?

She held her breath as a pair of heeled feet clicked on the hardwood floor toward them. Someone was coming.

Kiera glanced at Sally, who was putting the architectural book back on the shelf and moving to the shelf across from it where more scandalous novels rested. She made eye contact with Kiera, giving a look that said "It can't be Kent. He wouldn't wear heels."

Kiera imagined they both looked like deer caught in the headlights when a figure stepped into view, blocking the light partially behind her figure. It was a tall woman, wearing a tight skirt and buttoned-up shirt.

Kiera squinted at her, then breathed a sigh of relief. It was the librarian.

"What's she doing here?" Sally whispered as the librarian approached them. Did she want something from them? Or was she just looking for a book.

Kiera opened her mouth, ready to utter an

attack or invisibility spell at will, but she waited before doing anything rash.

The librarian walked right up to them, towering a head above them both, and peered over her glasses at their faces.

"Do you mind telling me what you two are doing in this aisle?" she asked, her tone a little off. She sounded more like a woman imitating a man, which wasn't normal for her. Kiera had spoken to her a few times and this wasn't like her.

"Are we not allowed to look at books in a library?" Sally asked, defensively placing her hand in front of the book Kiera was holding.

The librarian studied their faces a moment longer, then turned her attention to Kiera's book.

There was a moment of silence, then the woman snatched it out of Kiera's hands. Kiera gasped, making a sound of genuine embarrassment before feeling her cheeks turn pink. She wasn't sure if she should be scared or relieved that it was just the harlequin novel she'd been holding rather than the blueprints.

The librarian studied it, her brow furrowed. She still hadn't explained why she was spying on them like this.

"That's odd," she said thoughtfully. "I thought

books like this wouldn't be allowed in a school library."

"That's what I said," Kiera said quietly, all the while wondering why a librarian didn't know what type of books were on her own shelves.

Sally grabbed Kiera's arm and squeezed her, then spoke again with a confident voice.

"I got it off the shelf, I swear," Sally said, acting the part of a rebellious teenager trying to read something she wasn't supposed to. Anything to throw Kent or any other spies off the scent. "If you don't like the book, it shouldn't be here. Not my problem." She reached for the novel and the librarian didn't prevent her from taking it back.

"Hmm." There was another awkward silence as the librarian looked around at the shelves one more time, then sniffed. "As you were." Then she walked away, her manner of walking stiff and odd. Then, right before she reached the end of the aisle, her steps faltered before becoming natural again.

Sally released Kiera, then mouthed the words "I think that was Kent."

Kiera had suspected it and shuddered at the recent memory. Something had felt off from the start. She hated the thought of being controlled like that.

"High level spell," Sally mouthed. "Very danger-ous." Possession.

Kiera nodded. Message received. He was going to great lengths to spy on them now. He must be getting suspicious but couldn't be sure what they were doing. She seemed to recall hearing that too many memory wipes could scramble a person's mind, giving them permanent brain damage. It was unlikely he wanted to risk five kids all getting brain damage and an investigation being launched. So he was watching them and only planned to use the memory spell as a last resort.

"Alright, let's check out that book and go," Sally said, pointing at the book.

"Do I have to?" Kiera muttered.

"Of course. Then, we need to *go* to the *necro-mancy* building. I left one of my textbooks in the classroom and we need to go get it." She empha-sized certain words, though it was subtle enough that only Kiera would notice. "Also, Meiying had plans to go to the *staff* building to speak to one of the teachers about her grades. I promised I'd go cheer her on, so we should go there right after."

So, the oldest buildings and most likely candi-dates were the staff building and the necromancy building. Kiera wasn't surprised, since Kent's spooky classes took place in the basement of the necromancy building. The tunnels down there were dark and eerie, but she'd never thought they ran further than the reach of the building. At least she was familiar with that area. The staff building was more of an unknown and would have a lot of people asking why a pair of students were snooping around.

After they checked out the book, which made Kiera's face turn red as a tomato, they headed back outside to investigate. Sally took her time as they went, though, nonchalantly reading the harlequin book aloud as they went. If Kent was going to follow them around, he'd have to listen to Sir Reginald carrying Lady Diana on his horse back. It was only fair.

The necromancy building was, strangely, locked when they walked up to it. Kiera wasn't sure why. Teachers normally stayed after hours, either in the classroom or in their offices over in the staff building. It was odd that the doors were locked before eight.

It was probably Kent's doing, which made Kiera highly suspicious that *this* might be where they were needed to go.

"That's weird," Sally said but didn't press

further. "In that case, let's just grab Meiying and head to the staff building." Though now even Sally looked hesitant about leaving. If this wasn't a coincidence and the tunnels really did connect here, there was no point blowing their cover by sneaking into the staff building just to find absolutely nothing.

"Are you sure she needs you?" Kiera asked. "I think I remember Ben say he was going with her instead." Kiera was offering Sally a chance to back down and either tell the headmaster or at least rally reinforcements before they went in.

"You know what..." Sally didn't take long to think about it. "I don't much like hanging out with Ben, no offense. He's a major hassle on good days and he can get really clingy around Meiying. Maybe it's best to leave them to it." So, they were in agreement. The necromancy building was what they needed to focus on, and it might be best to give the impression that they'd given up so Kent wouldn't watch them too keenly. The librarian already made it clear that he was spying on us so it was best not to push their luck.

"Then I guess I'll go get my book tomorrow and risk Professor Stanley's wrath for being late," Sally said. She most likely hadn't forgotten a book at all and was lying. "Do you want to grab dinner? Or should we drop that book off at your dorm before we go?"

Kiera looked down at the harlequin book. Sally had handed it back to her after reading a full chapter during their walk. Frowning, she stuffed it inside her backpack. "No. It's not like anyone's going to be looking in my pack anyway. I'm hungry. Let's go." And hopefully meet up with the others.

Part of Kiera wished they had managed to get inside and confirmed their beliefs that the tunnels met up there. Delaying it was giving her more anxiety.

"Oh yeah, and that thing you mentioned earlier?" Sally said, continuing the conversation without skipping a beat. "I think we should meet up for it on Monday, after your special classes."

"Oh." They hadn't agreed to meet up for anything. This must be about... the necromancy building, where the special classes took place. Sally must be planning to meet up with Kiera in the basement with the others so they could look for a tunnel. "Right. Sounds good."

Sally smiled, a knowing grin of someone speaking a made-up language or sharing some great secret. "I'm glad we get to hang out like this, without the guys to interfere. I get to learn so much when I'm with you."

Like where the entrance to the tunnels might be. "Same here." They could only hope the locked door wasn't a coincidence and they weren't accidentally putting all their eggs in one basket. This had better be the right lead, otherwise Kent would figure them out and Ezra might be lost forever.

17

The next time Kiera had to enter the spirit realm for Kent's special classes, she found the location noticeably empty. There were no looming figures towering over her, there was no sign of Ezra or his fellow kidnapped students, and there wasn't even the familiar tug pulling her in a certain direction. It was just her, the orbs that represented various souls, and the feeling of Kent watching her. She couldn't see him but knew he was there.

Unsure what exactly he wanted her to do, since he just told her to practice entering and exiting the realm on her own, she made a show of looking around.

The location felt damp today, matching the cool air of the outdoors. She found that the realm slowly shifted overtime, sometimes appearing completely dark, sometimes shrouded with mist, and sometimes resembling a space full of stars.

Since she had a few minutes before she had to go back, she studied the souls surrounding her. There were the souls belonging to the other students in the class, some of them flickering nervously, while Kent's came in and out. It was like he chose when to look visible to her or not.

Strangely, there were four other souls moving past, about twenty feet away. They were fading in and out like Kent's was too. Who could—

Her heart, or what passed for one in this world, skipped a beat as she realized who those four were and what they were doing. That had to be Ben, Tucker, Sally, and Meiying investigating the basement while Kent was distracted with the class. Ben or Tucker must be shrouding their location somehow, which was why they sometimes appeared twenty feet away, then vanished and looked like they were much further back.

She turned away, not wanting to draw attention to them if Kent was looking. They hadn't discussed any plans with her—the less she knew, the better—which meant she'd have to adapt fast. If they *did* find the entrance and got it open, Kent would probably realize immediately. That meant they'd only have one shot at saving Ezra. If they succeeded, they'd be able to immediately bring him out and have evidence for the headmaster. If they failed, Ezra would probably banish or kill them, making it look like an accident.

Time was up. She had to go back.

Holding her breath, Kiera allowed herself to fall onto her back, uttering the spell to return her. Her body resisted the fall, since doing so normally could have resulted in a lot of pain, but she forced her body to obey and within three seconds was back in her chair, seated in the underground classroom. Kent was staring at her from his seat at the front, his eyes matching the flickering flames of the fireplace against the wall.

"Very good," he told her simply, then turned to the next student. "Andy, you're up next."

It took everything in her to avoid looking at the classroom door. She strained to hear her friends sneaking past but there was nothing. The only sound was the breathing of people beside her, the uttering of a spell by the next student in line, and Kent's chair scraping against the floor.

The rest of the class proceeded normally and Kiera spent the whole time repeating the spell to enter the spirit realm in her head over and over, hoping it would become muscle memory for her body. That way, even if her memory was wiped, her body could still recall it. It might prove useful in an emergency, especially if Kent tried to flee into the spirit realm forever if they won... which seemed unlikely, but still.

She noted how weak her body had become as she muttered the spell. Even though she was saying most of the spell under her breath, the magic around her barely moved. There was definitely less of it now and it felt weaker with each secret class. Kent was definitely weakening her and probably the other students too, stealing their magic. She was sure the thievery was related to the goddess of death, but she still didn't know what Vara planned to do with it.

Would Kiera eventually run out of magic? What would happen then? Would she die or would Kent finally kill her?

Once the hour ended and the students started packing up, Kiera's heart rate picked up and her hands were shaking as she grabbed her backpack. She was nearly tiptoeing as she headed for the door, but Kent's voice suddenly stopped her in her tracks.

"Kiera, I'd like to speak with you for a moment," he said from his seat.

She turned toward him, gulping. His arms were crossed and she could feel him analyzing her. Did he know her friends were down here poking around?

"Yes?"

"I'd like to invite your friend to my classes," he began, gesturing for her to sit again. "Ben, was it?"

Protectiveness flared up inside her. First Kent took her lover and now he wanted to drain her best friend too?

"I've heard he's a smart fellow, though a little eccentric and unmotivated. I'd like to teach him what I know. They always say to leave this world better than you left it, right? I need to share my knowledge while I'm still able."

Kiera didn't respond to that last part. "Ben isn't interested in necromancy. It creeps him out." Which was true.

"Oh. I thought you would have told him all the merits of necromancy and explained to him that there is more to necromancy than just death."

"I have," Kiera said honestly. "He doesn't like to listen. He's a stubborn guy." As in, he wouldn't make a good student. He didn't use a lot of magic anyway. He was just good at remembering and retaining spells. Half the time, Kiera felt him steal a bit of her magic to run his spells when he wasn't strong enough. He'd started doing it with Meiying too, as a partnership with consent, of course.

"Invite him over for our next class," Kent said, his voice deepening. He didn't seem amused by her honest talking down of Ben. He studied her again. "Are you not enjoying my classes?"

"I am," Kiera said slowly, uncomfortable. "They're interesting."

"But you don't want Ben to come."

"I just don't think he'll agree to it. He's quite headstrong."

Kent chuckled, turning away. Kiera didn't like the way his laugh sounded. It was like he knew more than he was letting on.

"Let him be the judge of that." He gestured for her to go. "Until next time, Miss Tully."

He hadn't called her that in a long while, at least not in that tone of voice. It felt like back in the day when there were no memories being stolen and Ezra was still with them. Did that mean he knew about her discovery?

"Goodbye, Professor Gillis," she said, making sure to use the polite name. Saying "Kent" would reveal things right away.

"Goodbye." He waved at her, though it was done dismissively. His patience had clearly run out.

She stepped outside the classroom, breathed a sigh of relief, then shut the door behind her.

As soon as the door was closed and she was

alone in the dark hallway with only a few artificial torches to tell her where she was going, a hand grabbed her from behind and a second one covered her mouth so she couldn't scream. In less than a second, she was pulled backwards into the darkness and deeper into the tunnel.

18

Kiera's gut reaction was to elbow whoever had grabbed her. She did so and heard a human grunt, male, which gave her relief. Her first thought had been of the goddess of death's tall, strong husband Kilon, who could snap her neck with just two fingers. This person was tall but not that tall. He also sounded just like Ben.

Kiera kept quiet as she was dragged backwards into the darkness. The view around her got fuzzy, either from blood rushing to her head or some type of magic Ben had cast. Once the tunnel was completely fuzzy, like she'd put on glasses that were the wrong prescription, Ben finally spoke.

"Sorry about that," he whispered and let her go. "Didn't want to risk Kent hearing us. He currently thinks we're hanging out in my dorm, playing videogames." He paused to mutter another spell, then added, "And now you're getting a phone call from me telling you to join us."

"You're getting good at this," Kiera muttered as she followed him further down the tunnel. "A little too good. If we make it out of this alive, I think we'll need to ban you from using that spell."

Ben chuckled as they reached the end where Tucker, Meiying, and Sally were waiting. They were all dressed in black and wearing backpacks.

"We found it," Sally told Kiera as soon as she reached them. "It's a concealed door but it's hidden by a tapestry, not any actual magic. Either he was really stupid or overconfident when it came to hiding this thing." To demonstrate, Sally pulled back the tapestry near the end of the tunnel. There were a few others on the wall nearby to help it blend in. The only difference between this tapestry and the others was that it depicted a beautiful, blonde goddess bearing a scythe and next to her was a red-haired man with a bow at his back and rippling muscles. It was Vara and Kilon. Kiera became enraged at how on the nose it was. If she hadn't been so afraid of this terrifying tunnel, she might have realized this obvious clue was here months ago.

"We're going in," Tucker said, his deep voice lined with agitation. "Meiying and Sally are going to stand watch. If something goes wrong, they'll run to the headmaster and tell him everything—if they can make it, that is."

"I thought you already told the headmaster," Ben said to Sally. "Or at least sent him a message."

"I did. I sent him a letter a week ago and didn't get a response, so I told my parents this time and they're on their way here. If we die, they'll tell everyone anyway."

"Why don't we just tell the headmaster now—" Kiera started but everyone shook their heads.

"You said we tried that already," Tucker said. "He'll erase all our memories. We only have one chance here. We can't squander it."

Kiera agreed. She just didn't like the fear that they might be acting stupid here. Sure, it felt like there was no other option than to just charge in before they ran out of time, but what if there was some other obvious solution they were missing?

There was no time to think it over. Meiying wished them luck, then Sally held the tapestry up so they could head inside. The square walls of the hallway were replaced by the round, naturally formed tunnels of old. There was an old, musty smell coming from within, as well as a damp wind that hinted at the tunnel descending even deeper into the earth. Kiera could now tell that the sense of being watched during her classes had come from this tunnel. The question was, who in here had been watching her?

"I'll keep my spell going as long as I can," Ben said as Kiera stood in front of the tunnel entrance. "But if I have to cast a new one, like if we're attacked, Kent will immediately know we're here, so try to be stealthy."

"We'll try to handle the spells," Tucker promised and Kiera nodded. "We've got your back."

Kiera shot Ben a thumbs up and he did it back to her. Then he gave Meiying a goodbye kiss.

"Take care of her," he told Sally, fulfilling the role of a good boyfriend.

Sally just laughed. "Sure, sure. Glad you're worried about *both* of us, Ben."

"You know what I mean." Ben turned toward his traveling companions, Tucker and Kiera. "So, who wants to go first?"

Kiera had never felt more eager to go into a terrifying, unknown location. The tug the goddess had given her was intense, practically begging her to go deeper. She could feel Ezra's presence now too and it was growing weaker. His life might be on a timer by now. There was no sense dawdling here because of a fear of the dark.

"I'll go," she said and stepped forward as Tucker created a magic light from his hand. "Let's hurry. I don't think we have much time left."

19

The tunnel got wider as they proceeded. Kiera went first, with Tucker right at her shoulder so he could light the way. Ben followed at the back, always extending the spells and doing little to help them in the tunnel. He just followed along like a blind grunt, relying on them completely for guidance.

About thirty feet in, Kiera felt Tucker's hand grip her shoulder and she stopped.

"What is it?" she whispered, scanning the tunnel.

"I just realized something from my high school DND days," he said. He must be referring to dungeons and dragons. "There are no long empty tunnels."

"Huh?" She wasn't sure where he was going with this.

Tucker gulped and started rifling through his book with his free hand. "There are always traps," he explained quietly.

Traps. Wonderful. Kiera shouldn't be surprised. Of course Kent wouldn't just leave a tunnel unprotected with only a tapestry to hide it. He was like a spider, waiting for innocent students to wander in and never come back out until they'd been drained of all magic and life they possessed.

"I have a spell to check for traps," Tucker explained quietly, then spoke a quick and easy spell that Kiera memorized. She then used it too.

The area around them lit up slightly. Everything became outlined in a blue glow and anything that required attention, like a trap or living creature, was outlined in red. It was like a videogame, but a little creepier because it made a dull hum and pulse fill her ears.

"Nothing here," Tucker said, "But we should keep the spells up the whole time we're in here."

"Of course." Obviously.

Kiera licked her lips and continued the spell as she took another step forward. More of the tunnel lit up ahead of them, as did a small wire running along the ground. It was a tripwire.

Kiera stopped, making Tucker stop too and Ben bumped into him a second later.

"What gives?" Ben hissed.

"Tripwire." Kiera looked above it, trying to figure out what it would have done to them had they stepped on it. "Up there. He has a net waiting to ensnare us."

"I'm surprised he used simple nonmagical items," Tucker commented as Kiera stepped forward. "It's too... easy."

"Maybe be—Whoa!" Kiera stifled a scream as she felt the ground beneath her feet shift, then the air felt like it leapt right out of her lungs as she fell forward onto her face. Stones scratched her cheeks and eyelids and her wrist stung from landing right on top of the taut string on the ground.

Wait, if her wrist just hit the tripwire, would it—

Her question was answered before she even finished her thought. The wire snapped, then she felt the heavy net crash onto her body. She never knew could feel so heavy and painful.

"I see," Tucker said, turning to Ben instead of helping Kiera as she craned her head to look up at them. "He used normal human traps as decoys so we wouldn't notice the magical traps."

"Are you two going to help me?" Kiera asked, eliciting a laugh from Tucker.

"Sorry. I was just doing it to mess around," he said as he pulled it off her. She felt the air come back into her lungs fully once she was free. "It's a good thing none of us came alone."

"So, what do we do about this? I'm sure the traps will get more lethal as we go," Ben said between spells. "He'll give up on capturing people and settle for killing them once they evade the first few traps."

"Kiera will have to look for human traps and I'll have to look for magical ones," Tucker answered. "It's a simple technique. We just have to stay on our toes."

So, they did just that. Kiera and Tucker walked side by side, going slowly, and Ben kept up his work behind them.

But then, Ben gasped.

"What is it?" Tucker asked, glancing over his shoulder.

Ben sighed and they felt the blurriness around them disappear. "Kent knows. He dispelled my magic."

"Shoot!" Kiera looked ahead, trying to gauge how far this tunnel went. "Should we make a run for it?"

"And get killed?" Tucker's voice cracked from nerves. "I don't know."

"We don't have any other options!" Ben shouted. "He's on his way here right now! We have to go! You two just keep an eye out!"

Tucker still looked hesitant but Kiera knew they couldn't let themselves die. If they made it this far after two memory wipes, Kent wouldn't let them go free again. It would be too risky.

"Run!" she shouted and did so. Ben followed quickly and Tucker grumbled but went with them too. He didn't keep his voice down as he spoke the spell this time. There was no need for stealth now.

"Right there!" Kiera shouted, pointing at a bear trap to the right. "A bear trap."

"And there's a magical warp hole next to it!" Tucker added. "Keep to the far left of the tunnel!"

"Right!" Ben and Kiera shouted. They did so and narrowly avoided the traps.

"Is it just me," Tucker asked another minute into their escapade, "or are we being watched?"

"I thought it was just me," Ben replied. "Yeah. I definitely feel something down here with us. Do you think the tunnel itself is alive? Also." Ben paused to cast a new spell, similar to the one Kiera just used. "Yup. Kent's on our tail."

Kiera felt her throat go dry. The very walls

around them might be alive, they were surrounded by traps they couldn't see, and there could be two immortal gods at the end of this tunnel, all while Kent chased them from behind. She couldn't imagine things getting any worse.

"Another trap!" Tucker warned, pointing right in front of them. "Dodge to the left or right!"

"Wait!" Kiera hadn't kept her spell going long enough. She started shouting the words, ignoring how much it stung her dehydrated throat. She had enough time to cast the spell and warn them. "Just wait a second. I need to check for normal traps."

"We don't have time to slow down!" Ben warned.

"I know, I—" She finished the spell but instead of improving her vision so she could see everything clearly in the dark, her sight went darker instead. The spell had failed. How? She said everything correctly!

The magic around her was dragging on the ground, like it had been pushed beyond its limits. It was akin to a weak animal, exhausted from a long run. This had never happened before. Her magic was always strong enough to keep her going. She hadn't made a mistake like this since her first semester!

Oh, no. She knew what happened.

"Kiera!" Tucker shouted. "Right or left!" They only had a few more feet to go and she didn't have time to cast the spell again. There was no space to slow down either.

"I—" She could barely see now. A stone hit the front of her foot and she nearly fell forward, right into the magical trap. She didn't know what to do.

Kent had been draining her magic for weeks. Now there was too little of it left and she'd over-worked what little she had remaining. It was common knowledge that you shouldn't use too much magic all at once, but her limits had been lowered so much that she hadn't had time to adjust. Now it was backfiring.

"Go either way!" Tucker ordered, taking over. It was clear she couldn't handle this anymore.

Kiera leapt to the right while Tucker and Ben dove to the left. If they were lucky, there wouldn't be any traps on either side, but if they weren't...

❦ 20 ❦

Kiera felt herself fly through the air, her head going first and arms right after. She heard Tucker and Ben leap next to her, then they grunted as they landed on the dirt. They were safe.

She wasn't so lucky.

Kiera could only grunt as a steel bar swung out from the wall and hit her squarely in the chest, sending pain between her ribs and making warm blood immediately trail down her front to the ground. Her arms and head dangled over the bar, then it swung back against the wall and she fell onto, only just now realizing there had been spikes on that bar too. They'd cut right through her skin, luckily not hitting any bones or organs but still going deep enough to bleed.

The ground felt very nice as she collapsed onto it, tempting her to fall asleep, but then the pain overwhelmed it. She was barely able to feel Ben grab her and pull her away so the bar couldn't get triggered again and hit her a second time.

"Help me," she whispered, feeling blood travel up her throat and clog it. She felt the last of her magic pressing up against her like cats rubbing against their master. If it had any power left, she needed it to heal her one last time.

"Help you? What do you *think* I'm doing?" Ben shouted at her, then scoffed as he looked over his shoulder. "I see him. It's Kent. Tucker!"

"I see him too!" Tucker shouted. He said a quick spell while Ben dashed down the tunnel, Kiera still in his arms. His feet bound over the ground unnaturally quickly and Tucker stayed right beside him. Tucker must have cast a speed spell on them both.

"Please," Kiera implored one more time. She could almost see the magic pressing against her ribs now. It resembled a white mist that shifted into a variety of shapes and animals. "Please save me."

"Is she dying?" Tucker shouted.

"No!" Ben looked over his shoulder again and swore. "He's getting closer."

"Stop looking back and run!" Tucker screamed back.

Kiera tried to pull herself up slightly so she could see over Ben's shoulder. Then she regretted it immediately. Kent was sprinting toward them, even faster than Ben and Tucker were going. He was shouting spells as he went, the words dark and unnatural. They sounded more like growls and hisses than human sounds. It sounded like death magic, but far greater than anything she had ever learned.

"He's trying to... kill us," she whispered. "His spells—"

"Yeah, I kind of gathered that!" Ben shouted back at her.

She smirked, pushing through the pain to think of a cheeky comeback.

All of a sudden, the pain in her abdomen vanished. Looking down, she saw the last of the mist start to fade away. The remains of her magic had healed her, even though she hadn't said a spell.

"Wait." She could now feel the magic leaving her completely, going out like a flame at the bottom of a candle that had burned for too long. She'd finally used it all up... and now she regretted it. She'd had no choice but she didn't want to lose it completely. "Don't go."

The magic fluttered in front of her face for a

final moment, resembling a tiny moth, then it completely fizzled out. It was gone.

Kiera's chest seized with a longing and loneliness, just like how she felt when Ezra was taken from her. Kent had taken another treasured thing she depended on. Her magic was permanently gone. Now she'd be useless.

"I can move," she told Ben. "I'm healed. You can let me go now."

"Nah," Ben said, nodding ahead of them. There was a light at the end of the tunnel now. They were almost out. "Faster to just keep going. Use a spell to save us if you're well enough to run your mouth now."

"I can't," Kiera said, losing her voice. "I'm sorry." She had lost her magic for good.

Realization came over Ben's face, then he immediately started shouting complicated words of his own. This must be high magic he was spouting.

"I'm feeling weaker," Tucker warned them. As soon as he said it, their speed slowed down. Kent was probably taking their magic for himself, alongside trying to weaken them enough to kill them. He was building up his power before using a huge attack. How cliché... and terrifying.

"Get in here!" Tucker shouted, crossing the

threshold into the lit up area at the end of the tunnel.

Ben complied and tossed Kiera right through the opening. Then he immediately turned around and raised his hands over his head. Kiera landed on her knees and felt them scrape against a stone floor. Then she turned around, expecting to see Kent murder Ben. Instead, she saw Ben holding up a blue barrier in front of the tunnel, blocking the villain.

"I don't know how long I can hold this!" Ben warned as Kent finally reached them. His eyes were literally red and his mouth was raised in a horrifying sneer. Kiera squinted and realized there were scales on his arms too. He really was powering himself up.

"Why didn't he kill us?" Kiera whispered, confused by Kent's strange actions, especially now that he'd stopped behind the shield and wasn't doing anything to counter it. "He had a lot of time to do it in that tunnel."

"Why kill us when he could drain the last of our magic first?" Tucker muttered, glaring at the now still but equally frightening Kent before turning away and scanning the massive room they'd just entered.

There was a reason Kent wiped their memories rather than kill them right away. He needed their magic and couldn't get it if they were dead. He probably planned to use their souls as puppets later too. Killing them would be easy but useless. The question was: What did he plan to do with all that magic?

"We need to hurry and find Ezra!" Kiera shouted to Ben. "How long can you give us?"

"We don't need any time," Tucker cut in before Ben could answer. "Ezra's right here."

"What?"

Before she turned around to see what Tucker was talking about, Kiera made eye contact with Kent one more time. His now crimson eyes looked her up and down, like he was appraising her. It wasn't the first time he'd looked at her like that. Then, after giving Ben's shield one more tap, he smirked and vanished right in front of their eyes.

"He gave up just like that?" Ben asked. "I'm surprised. Did we overestimate him?"

Kiera shook her head. "He'll be back. We can't let our guard down yet."

"Kiera," Tucker pleaded, already running away from her toward whatever he had seen. "Hurry."

Doing as he asked, Kiera turned around. As

soon as she did, her heart lit up. It was him—the person they'd spent months looking for.

Kiera, Ben, and Tucker had found themselves inside a large dome, buried underground for maybe a hundred years. It was formed from stone but had some golden inlays along certain edges and the doorframes. At the top, Kiera could see a hole with water magically flowing in a circle. That must connect to the water fountain in the campus plaza. To think, after all this time, she could have just jumped into the fountain and found her way in here a long time ago. How frustrating.

There was another door at the far end of the dome, leading into an identical tunnel opposite the one they just left. Guarding each side of this door was a pair of statues standing at attention in full armor. One was a woman, tall and beautiful with roman plates, and the other was a male, wearing animal skins and bones woven into his hair. Kiera was pretty sure she knew who those two were. The bigger question was who built statues for them. Did someone, a hundred years ago, become as obsessed with Vara and Kilon as Kent was?

All of these surroundings were noteworthy, but the most important part of this room, and the thing Kiera zeroed in on immediately, was a group of hooded figures huddled in the center of the dome. There were five of them and they were kneeling on the floor in a small circle.

Tucker was already running toward them, arms outstretched to pull the hoods from their heads.

Kiera's heart leapt. There were five figures and five missing students. This was the spot where Vara's gift had led her—where Ezra was supposed to be. One of those figures must be him.

Part of her worried this might be a trap, but since Tucker still had his scanning spell on as far as she knew, if there was something amiss, he would know about it. Since he didn't seem worried, Kiera decided she wouldn't be either and ran after him. If this didn't end up being Ezra, she'd be devastated.

Tucker reached the first person and pulled off their hood, revealing a pale woman with greasy, unwashed hair, sunken cheeks, and wide eyes that stared at the wall. She didn't look toward Tucker until he spoke, asking her name.

"Her name's Cindy," Kiera whispered. She'd gotten close enough to see her face. "She was a student in Kent's class."

Tucker's face lit up and he started pulling off all the hoods. The second was one of the top students who loved asking questions, the next was a naturally talented boy who wasn't good at memorizing but had a magical connection as strong as Kiera's.

The fourth was another girl, and the final one was a thin, sickly Ezra. His pupils were huge when Tucker pulled off the hood, but as soon as he made eye contact with Kiera, they crinkled in a soft, tired smile.

"You found me," he whispered, his voice croaky and quiet as could be, but filled with joy at the sight of her. Then he chuckled, as though all his tensions had finally been released, and looked up at Kiera and Tucker. "Took you long enough."

"**D**id I hear that correctly?" Ben shouted from the entrance. He was still holding up the shield, probably paranoid Kent would come back. Kiera doubted he would and if he did, he wouldn't waltz through the entrance like that when he could teleport or use some other means. "Did he just complain about us being too slow? Maybe we should leave him here, Kiera," he joked, making a few of the already drained students pale.

"I'm sure Kiera will tell him off for us," Tucker said, grinning, the tension leaving his shoulders and letting them droop.

"Can any of you stand?" Kiera asked, still expecting Kent to suddenly appear behind her with a knife and stab her with it. "There's only three of us."

"Right. No more chatter. Those of you who can walk, please stand up. Those who can't, we'll try to carry or help."

One of the boys and girls was well enough to limp, but Ezra and other two could barely stand without slumping over, so Kiera put her arm under Ezra's shoulder while Ben and Tucker helped the other two. Then, it was time to decide what to do next.

"Do you think Meiying and Sally are okay?" Ben asked nervously as they stood in the center of the dome. "Kent had to get past them to reach us, right?"

"I didn't see any blood on him," Tucker said. "So there's a chance they slipped away without him realizing they were there."

"Let's hope," Ben muttered, worried about his girlfriend. "Which way should we go? Through the new door or back through the traps?"

Kiera bit her lip, feeling Ezra's weight get heavier on her shoulder. He looked ready to fall asleep then and there. She could barely feel any magic around him too. Kent had been draining him down here for months, probably waiting for his magic to return to him or replenish before stealing more of it again.

Should they try the new tunnel? It might lead somewhere dangerous. However, none of these students would be able to traverse those areas. One of them would definitely step into one by accident, through no fault of their own.

"Let's try the back tunnel," she told the others, nodding at it even though the statues of the gods scared her. "Can one of you check the tunnel first to make sure there's nothing worse down there?"

"Well, it is leading upwards," Ben commented as Tucker started casting a couple spells to see what lay ahead. "It's probably a back entrance. No one makes a place underground without a second entrance. Cave-ins mandate it."

"Looks safe," Tucker said. "Just a few traps and I can trigger them before we go."

"Wait, you can trigger them?" Ben cut in. "Why didn't you do that on the way here?"

"In case you forgot, we were in a rush and also didn't want to tip Kent off," Tucker said dryly between spells. They heard a few clicks and snaps further down the tunnel, then Tucker stopped casting. "Plus, it's risky to set off traps without knowing what they're going to do. If we didn't have wounded with us, I would have suggested we try sneaking around them instead."

"Can we debate this while we walk?" Kiera interrupted, desperately wishing she could use a healing spell on Ezra. She missed her magic more than ever. If only she could draw the magic of others to herself and use that instead... though that wasn't too different from what Kent had been doing. Stealing wasn't a great idea, especially after everything they'd been through.

"I agree," Ezra wheezed, squeezing Kiera tighter like he was afraid she'd disappear from him again. "Let's go. I'd rather listen to you two yell at each other in a place that isn't a prison."

"Agreed," one of the other students said.

Argument concluded, they headed forward, with Ben at the front and Tucker at the rear. That way, if Kent attacked from either side, they'd have a magic user to defend them. No mention was made of Kiera's lost magic. She was sure most of them could feel her loss, either physically or due to how heartbroken she looked despite finally reuniting with her love. It felt like a hole had been carved inside her and could never be refilled.

The tunnel was longer but, thanks to Tucker's magic disabling all the traps ahead of them, they were able to go through safely, albeit slowly. All the people they'd rescued were limping or being carried and they slowed the group down considerably. The five minute dash from the first tunnel changed into a twenty minute walk down this second one. It didn't help that they were all wary of Kent's return. At least in the previous chase, they'd known where Kent was. Now he could pop up at any moment and cave the tunnel in on them and they wouldn't have time to react.

"I missed you," Ezra whispered in Kiera's ear as they walked, making her jump because she was so on edge. "I was starting to worry he killed you."

The fear in his voice filled her with remorse that she hadn't tried harder. He had been imprisoned by his own brother and drained continually with the knowledge that he could die at any moment, yet he'd spent that time worrying about her instead.

"I was looking for you," she assured him, equally quiet and wishing she had water to give him or at least a spell that could do it. "But Kent kept wiping our memories every time we got close. If it weren't for our meeting in the spirit realm, we might never have found you."

He grinned half-heartedly. "I spent half my time

in there with those... things." He shuttered. "The gods he mentioned. They were sucking up my life force like I was some animal bred for their pleasure His words were filled with revulsion at the memory. "The days I was able to cling to you in the spirit world were all that kept me alive."

So it *had* been his spirit following her after all, though reality had kept them physically split. "We won't be apart again," she assured him. She didn't know how to keep that promise but she'd die before she lost him again.

"I wanted to tell you," he continued, his eyes dimming as sleep threatened to overtake him. "Before I died, I wanted to tell you I loved you. I'm saying it now. There were so many times I regretted pushing you away."

Kiera gulped, not sure if this was the best time but he probably wanted to do it in case something happened to them.

"I thought I was protecting you," he continued, "by refusing to let you get too close. I worried Kent would put a target on you, though it looks like he ended up doing that anyway."

"He did." It helped to know that Ezra had been thinking about her all this time. Meanwhile, she'd been angry at him for never pursuing a rela- tionship with her. Only a couple times had she considered the idea that Ezra was doing it to keep her safe. "Thank you for looking out for me, Ezra."

She wanted to say she loved him too but before she could, Ben spoke up from the front of the line.

"I'm seeing a bit of light. I think we're almost free."

"Famous last words!" Tucker called back, trying to lighten the mood. Ben matched it by shouting back for Tucker to shut up before using a spell to make sure the door in front of him, which Kiera could barely see, was safe to open. It appeared to be a simple, wooden door angled slightly upwards. The tunnel they'd been following went at a slight incline but it must not have been enough, hence the door had to accommodate for it by a having a few steps below the door.

"I'm opening it," Ben announced before waving his hand. He didn't even have to touch the door. He cast a spell instead, allowing the knob to turn and swing open on its own accord. It revealed a familiar forest before them with the sun just beginning to descend. It was getting late.

"We're east of the campus, I think," Ben commented. He hesitated, glancing past the other students at Kiera. She gave him a nod, praying Kent wasn't waiting outside for them. Then, Ben stepped out into the open air again. Nothing happened. It was safe.

"Let's keep moving," Tucker said. "I've already sent a message to the headmaster and police but we still don't want to get caught out here after dark."

The other students didn't need more prodding. They were eager to escape the damp walls they'd been trapped in for months. By the time Kiera and Ezra reached the door, most of the other students were out and staring at the sky like this was their first time seeing it. Their pale faces got a bit of color back into them, reacting to the cold breeze blowing between the trees. A few of them cracked smiles despite their exhaustion. They were out!

The rest of the daylight became a blur as soon as the group walked back to the campus. They did so with little difficulty thanks to Ben's natural navigation skills and Tucker's compass spell. As soon as they set foot on the school grounds, they saw a flurry of people darting about—some were students and teachers but many were normal and magical police officers. All eight of them stopped as soon as they reached the edge of the crowd. Ben glanced at Kiera, who shrugged. They weren't quite sure what was going on, though they could venture a guess.

"Excuse me." Tucker grabbed the nearest student and gestured toward all the men and women in black and blue uniforms running past. "What's going on?"

"One of the professors was caught kidnapping students," the unknown young man answered without hesitation. "But I heard the perp got away and no one's found the students yet."

"Ah." Tucker glanced back at the students, raising an eyebrow in amusement. They were about to get a warm welcome. "Ben."

"What?"

"I think Meiying and Sally reached the headmaster after all. The police wouldn't have had enough time to get here from my message alone," Tucker explained.

Relief washed over Ben's face at the news that his girlfriend was probably okay.

"Well then," Ezra spoke up, taking charge even though he could barely walk. He looked each fellow victim in the eye. "Let's tell them everything that happened. Maybe we can help them catch Kent."

"Way ahead of you." Ben broke off from the group to get a police officer's attention. As soon as everyone realized who they were and that they were the ones everybody was looking for, the already chaotic campus became a mad house. There were shouts, cheers, gasps, and even sobs at the sight of the emancipated, drained students, as well as outrage at the teacher who had done this to them.

Kent was a wanted man now and there wasn't a single spell big enough to wipe every single person's memory of his crimes.

23

As paramedics rushed in ten minutes later to check Kent's victims for wounds and to help with their malnutrition, Kiera found herself pushed back from her friends and eventually shoved off to the side. As she was enveloped by the crowd of students and staff trying to see what was going on, she saw Ezra wave goodbye to her before he disappeared from sight behind the mass of bodies. He was being given an IV and looked a little more alert now that they were safe.

Glad that he was in good hands, she turned her attention to finding Tucker and Ben again, who had been swept off as well. Ben was nowhere to be seen, though she assumed he'd run off to find Meiying as soon as he could. Tucker was in sight, though. He was speaking to the headmaster at the edge of the crowd and seemed to be speaking harshly, which wasn't like him. The stressful situation had brought out a few sides of him Kiera rarely got to see.

She was just debating whether to join them when the headmaster himself, Ezra's uncle, spotted her and waved her over. There was no escaping him now.

"I'm glad all of you are safe," Charles Phil Gillis told her as soon as she joined them. "And I'm so sorry I couldn't be of more help. Both of you did a very brave thing and I'm ashamed to say that this is the third time you've done something I should have been doing myself."

He sounded genuine and Kiera felt bad for not giving him fair warning beforehand. In her defense, there was considerable risk when it came to alerting the headmaster, and there'd always been a tiny chance that he wasn't even on their side, but she still felt guilty. The headmaster had been searching for Ezra too, not believing Kent's lies about a "family trip" and suspecting Kent of kidnapping from the get-go, but without evidence, there was nothing he could realistically do. That helplessness was written all over his face even now.

"Well, what matters is that's he's safe," Kiera began, trying to reassure him.

The headmaster nodded, then his expression hardened. "But Tucker tells me Kent disappeared."

"Yes." Kiera was glad they were addressing that right away.

"Rest assured that we have everyone in both the normal and magical force searching for him. I will not rest until he's caught and brought to justice. That's why I called you over, Ms. Tully. Do you know of any clues that might help us know where he went? Tucker says you attended special necromancy classes that only a few other students went to. Is there anything he did or taught you that might help us find his current location?"

She frowned, hating that empty gap in her memory. "All I know is he taught us about the spirit realm and how to enter it and I only remember that part because it happened in my dreams. I can't remember what exactly was taught in the classes beyond that."

"Can't remember?" The headmaster furrowed his brow.

"He wiped their memory at the end of every class," Tucker explained quickly. "Said it would prevent their minds from getting overloaded."

"Well, that's highly illegal," the man commented, frowning as he thought it through. "The spirit world. Is there anything he specifically wanted you to do in there?"

"I think he was just using it to drain our magic and take it for himself," Kiera said, then quickly explained what she'd learned about the goddess Vara and her husband Kilon. "I think he was working together with them."

"You don't look surprised," Tucker commented, referring to the headmaster, who was listening intently. "Is this not his first time doing something like this?"

"Unfortunately, no." The headmaster sighed. "When we were much younger, as I'm sure you heard, he got into similar trouble. He's always been drawn to power. I hoped he would change, we all did, but he has taken this second chance and squandered it."

It felt a little uncomfortable for Kiera to hear such a personal family matter brought into the light, especially when it was clear there were a lot of painful feelings and trauma attached to it.

"Rest assured," the headmaster finished, "Once we find him, he'll be locked away for good. If you two see anything suspicious, let me know. Oh, and I've called your parents. They'll be arriving tomorrow to check up on you, though we'll be keeping all of you on campus for now, just in there are any more magical attacks."

Kiera cringed at the thought of her father's worrying. Her mother was used to magic being abused but all of this was constantly new and terrifying in her father's eyes, since he never used magic.

"Now, if you'll excuse me, I'd like to go check on my nephew." The headmaster stepped past them, looking absolutely miserable. "Thank you again. I don't know what we'd do without you two."

"And Benjamin Lord," Tucker added. "Without him, we never would have succeeded."

"I'll be sure to make a note of it." There. He finally smiled. "You three have a strong future ahead of you. I'll see to it you're rewarded for all you've done in the last two years."

Kiera's chest swelled with pride.

"Just swear to me you won't allow pride or fear to overcome you as Kent did," were his final words before he left them. "I've seen enough squandered potential in one lifetime."

Tucker beamed at Kiera and gave her a hug, thanking her for persisting when the rest of them couldn't. Then they both took a seat on the bench, getting a much needed break before meeting up with Ben, Meiying, and Sally again.

The work was done. The fight was over. They'd won and Kent was a fugitive. Kiera should be the happiest girl in the world.

But she couldn't shake the feeling that this wasn't over yet.

24

The paramedics and investigators didn't stop treating the victims and searching for Kent well into the darker hours of the day. So, while Kiera remained on the bench, waiting for Ezra to be released from the healers, the others headed out to eat or call their parents and assure them everything was okay. Kiera considered doing the same, but since her parents were supposedly on their way here anyway, she figured there was no harm in waiting until then. Besides, she wanted to be there for Ezra as soon as he got out. He would need the comfort after everything he'd been through. Hopefully his parents would come to check on him too as soon as they heard what happened from the headmaster.

While she sat on the cold bench, wrapped in a

blanket one of the police officers had given her and allowing her short legs to swing off the edge, she waited for her magic to return to her. Her insides ached without them, like a hunger deep inside her stomach that couldn't be filled with food. Now that she had time to sit here in silence, she could feel the slightest inkling that the magic still existed, just elsewhere. Someone, probably Kent or Vara, had taken it but it still existed, waiting for her to find and retrieve it.

Yet without magic to cast a sensing spell, she had no way of knowing where it was.

Tears pricked her eyes as she stared at the ground, wishing Kent had been more like his little brother instead. She'd rather face deadly fairies or dragons or trolls. Anything was better than a a thief.

"For a woman who's just become revered as a hero, you don't look too happy."

Her head shot up at the sound of Ezra's voice and she finally got to see him again, standing in front of her with an identical blanket wrapped around his shoulders. He still looked sickly and beyond skinny so she could see his bones protruding from his skin, but his eyes had life in them again. They still shone, flirtatious and teasing despite the trauma.

"Are you okay?" she asked, all thoughts of her lost magic gone. "Should I get someone—"

"I'm fine," he whispered, sitting beside her and hesitantly resting his head on her shoulder. "I just want to see you. Don't summon anyone else."

Now that her own magic was no longer around to distract her, she could sense the magic of others. She could feel his magic still intact, though it was weak and barely surviving.

"I lost my magic," she admitted.

"To Kent?"

"Yeah." She sighed, blowing her hair out of her face and enjoying the feel of Ezra's weight on her shoulder. "And he's still out there."

"I know. My uncle searched the tunnels himself and found no sign of him, though they did find a lot of skeletons in some secret caverns below the dome where we sat." He shuddered. "We weren't the first students Kent has killed. Uncle Phil was furious."

Kiera's stomach twisted in disgust. "I don't think Kent was the first one to do something like this." The goddess had been enlisting necromancers for years. "It might not have been him."

"Doesn't matter either way." Ezra's voice was tinged with malice. "He tried to kill us and needs to be locked away so he can't do it again."

"I agree." The question was how. She had no

magic and Ezra's was weak. Even Tucker and Ben had lost a bit of theirs during the chase, though they hadn't had to spend months in proximity to Kent, so theirs was still intact. "Do you think we should team up with the others and hunt your brother down?"

"My uncle wouldn't forgive us if we did," Ezra said, "But it wouldn't be the first time we did that, right?"

Kiera allowed herself to laugh, glad Ezra was finally back to his old self. Without Kent to drag him down, he was allowed to joke around and relax without the weight of his family name on his shoulders. She'd missed him so much.

"Let's worry about that tomorrow," Ezra added. "Right now, I just want to sleep."

"On this bench?" Kiera didn't like the sound of that.

"Yes. On this bench, in the cold with all these people around." Ezra laughed at her and got to his feet before offering to help her up too. "I'll have to ask for your help again. I... don't think I can walk all that way."

"Sure." It was nice to have him depend on her just this once. She was sure within a month; he'd be stronger than her again.

Ezra didn't talk much during their walk to the

dorms and he was so tired by the time they arrived that Kiera walked him right to his room. As soon as they were inside, he collapsed onto the bed and fell asleep without even saying goodnight.

Kiera stared at him for a good amount of time, not wanting to leave him after she'd worked so hard to get him back. There was a voice in the back of her head warning her that Kent was still out there and might try to snatch Ezra up while he slept. An image of him teleporting in and shoving Ezra back into the spirit world dominated her mind.

So, after only a little deliberation, she decided to curl up next to him in the bed and guard him all night. There wasn't much she could do without her magic, but just being next to him made her feel better. He'd probably hate to wake up to an empty room anyway.

As she stared at his gaunt but still handsome face and thought about how he needed a shower, she finally let it sink in that he was here. He wasn't a fading memory anymore. He was alive and next to her and had even told her he loved her. All this time, he had trusted that she'd find him. Now that she had him, she would never let him go again. Once his eyes opened, she'd return his confession and they'd promise to look after each other forever from this day forward.

She wiped a stray hair from in front of his eyes, then settled down to rest. The first hour was spent in paranoia, sitting up at every creak and opening her eyes whenever the wind beat against the window, but eventually she fell asleep to empty dreams. They were thankfully devoid of Kent and the goddess, no longer dragging her back into the spirit realm and trapping her there so they could suck away the last of her life. They couldn't torture her tonight. This moment was too perfect to ruin. Plus, she had nothing more to offer them, so there was no benefit to torturing her again.

By the time morning came, she hoped her magic would return and Kent would be caught by the headmaster. Then she could graduate in peace.

25

When Kiera snapped awake, her gut reaction was that someone had woken her. Sitting up immediately, she searched the room, expecting to see Kent at the foot of Ezra's bed like he was when he wiped her memory. Instead, she saw nothing but a messy bedroom. The drawers were still opened and papers scattered from when she, Ben, and Tucker had gone through the space to find clues. There was no evil necromancer crouching in the corner, waiting to cast a spell on her. Instead, she realized with a start that the sound of birds outside the window had been what woke her. They chirped again, loud and high pitched. She was so used to being on edge that even a slight chirp could wake her, it seemed.

Sighing and letting her head fall back onto

Ezra's second pillow, she turned to look at him. He was still asleep, breathing slowly. Now that light was streaming in, she could see the cuts and bruises on his face more clearly. They were brown and yellow, meaning they had to be at least a few days old. How many times had Kent struck him? Her blood boiled. Kent had taken his jealousy and resentment so far without anyone to stop him.

After allowing herself to drink in the sight of Ezra for a minute or two, she became aware of how creepy she was being and decided it was best to get out of bed. She turned to look out the window at the school grounds and was unsurprised to see a mass of people on the walkways despite how early it was. There were teachers, police officers, students, and even a few men and women wearing long, black robes. Those last ones were a new arrival. Headmaster Gillis must have summoned some high level magicians to come help. If Kent was still on the grounds, they'd be able to find him.

But what if he wasn't on the grounds anymore? He had disappeared right before their eyes, which meant he either teleported away or hopped right into the spirit world, physical body and soul together. Kiera wasn't sure if that was possible but knew Kent hadn't taught her everything in those classes. It could happen.

Ezra rolled over in his bed and it made Kiera turn back to him, unable to prevent a grin from overtaking her. She was watching the man she loved sleep. This was a moment she'd dreamed of for over a year and now it was happening.

"I love you too," she whispered across the room to him, hoping her voice would drift through his sleepy mind and right into his dreams.

The romantic moment over, she sat on the edge of the windowsill, texting Ben to ask him what the plans were. Classes were definitely canceled but if they were all quarantined on this land with magicians sweeping the grounds, the cafeteria was definitely not closed.

She was just typing the last word when she felt her balance shift, like she was about to fall off the windowsill and to the ground below. But that wasn't possible. The window was closed.

The phone slipped from her fingers as she realized that it wasn't her body falling. It was her soul.

She was falling back into the spirit world one last time.

Kent had finally played his last card.

❄ 26 ❄

Kiera blinked and found herself back in the world of the spirits. A dark figure stood in front of her, shrouded in shadow, but within two more blinks, his identity was revealed from the glow of the ground beneath their feet. It was Kent, though he no longer looked like the teacher she first met. He was completely corrupted now, his skin black and charred, his eyes a bright red with a slight glow about them. His mouth was twisted up in a smirk and a snarl, revealing teeth that shouldn't be as sharp as they were.

"I hope you enjoyed your last moments of freedom," he muttered, his voice a hiss similar to that of the goddess Vara. "Now I can finally have my revenge for you being such an annoying little prick throughout the year." The tone shifted back into normal Kent again. "You have no idea how frustrating it was to have to invite you to those classes and act all friendly while I wanted to wring your neck."

"Calm down, human." Goddess Vara's voice slipped into the conversation, monotone but calm and collected. Kiera turned to see the massive woman standing to her right, and another twist of the head revealed Kilon to her left. She was boxed in and didn't know how to leave. If she had the knowledge on how to escape, she could flag down the magicians outside Ezra's window and warn them that Kent had been hiding in the spirit world all along, just as she suspected.

She didn't know how to leave, though, not without Kent's help.

"Then hurry it up," Kent growled, not taking his eyes off Kiera as he addressed Vara. "And don't kill her completely. I want that honor."

"Don't be such a baby." Vara chuckled, then grunted as she roughly grabbed Kiera's hand. Even though Kiera's body flitted in and out of a physical form, the pain of Vara's fingers squeezing her wrist never abated. With the normal pain came a burning sensation within her chest and it spread. It felt like rot eating away at her. Kiera gasped as realization came over her. Now that she had no more magic to offer her, they were draining her life instead. That was why Kent was so eager to have the final blow. They were killing her.

Kilon grabbed her too and she didn't have the strength to utter a word. It felt like her jaw had rotted off. Part of her wished her eyes would do the same so she could stop having Kent in her view. His eyes were wide with glee, his mouth open in a grin as he anticipated her end.

Kiera thought this moment couldn't get any worse until she saw another person slip into view. It was one of the new girls from Kent's secret class. She nearly tripped as she came in, shrieking in confusion as she looked around. Then she became rooted in place, her arms at her sides like every part of her had become frozen except her face, which was now contorted into a horrified expression of pure fear.

Kent snapped his finger a few times. With each snap or swing of his hand, another student came into view. Some of them were the thin victims of his earlier imprisonment, while others were students who still went to the classes at the same time Kiera did without Ezra.

He was bringing them in to steal their lives and

use it to bring Vara and Kilon back to life. That had to be it.

Kiera wanted to cry, to punch these two gods in a last ditch effort to escape, but she was immobilized like the rest of the incoming students. The only thing she could do was sit here, waiting... and feel the presence of her magic.

Yes, she felt her magic again. It had such a distinct feeling that she couldn't miss it. It was nearby too. Was it—

She turned her head toward the goddess to confirm her suspicions. Her guess was right. Her magic was mingled in with the other ones floating around the goddess, under her control. The woman had an intense amount of it around her, more than was normal. This must be what she'd taken from all the students here, as well as probably a century's worth of other victims. It sickened Kiera to think that Vara and Kilon had probably taken over a hundred people's magic and lives, all so they could bring their two souls back to life. So many souls had been lost for a mere two to come back. It was beyond selfish.

The last student brought in was Ezra, who looked half asleep before he realized what was happening and tried to leap toward Kiera to protect her. His hand was a few inches away from hers when Kilon released Kiera and grabbed Ezra instead, yanking him aside and draining the last of his magic instead. Ezra screamed from the pain, then whirled on his brother.

"Kent! You can put a stop to this! You can still fix all the wrong things you've done by helping us now!" he shouted, his voice filled with the desperation of a young boy who used to idolize his brother and wish he could become like him.

Kiera saw Kent's smile twitch, like he was finally feeling doubts like a normal person for once. Then his smile widened and Kiera realized it was amusement, not doubt, that had made him twitch. "I'm sorry brother. I wish you'd been smarter. If you were, you would have joined me."

Ezra must have seen it too, because he stopped struggling then and looked down at the pitiful man that used to be his brother. "Then my brother is truly dead. Uncle Phil was right to give up on you. I tried to convince him that you were trying to make things right. Now I see that I should have listened to him all along." And just like that, the last shred of hope that Kent would become good once more completely faded from Ezra's eyes. He knew Kent was beyond saving and would tear himself apart following a goddess whose only power was murder.

Kiera looked at Kent once more. Whereas a

moment ago, she hadn't seen a shred of humanity in him, now she did. For a split second, she thought she saw remorse in his eyes, loss at what could have been.

Then it was gone. He was back to the power hungry, barely human beast who was willing to slaughter children to get what he wanted.

"Fine by me," Kent said. "I seem to recall telling you once that you shouldn't trust anyone. Shame on you for not listening to me." His cliché lines over, he fashioned a chair out of nothing and sat on air, reclining as Kilon and Vara drained Ezra and Kiera. Kiera could feel her very insides eating away at themselves and drifting toward Vara, giving her the strength and flesh she wanted to fashion her own body.

"It's enough," Vara suddenly said and released Kiera. "That's all we need."

"What?" Kent nearly fell back in his invisible chair, pointing at Kiera. "There's more you can take from her!"

"I don't want to waste these two just yet," Vara said softly, looking Kiera and Ezra over with an appraising nod. "We'll come back to them if we need them. Exercise a little patience, Kent."

With that, Kiera felt her flesh and bone return to her as a shockwave sent her, Ezra, and all the other students tumbling backwards. They fell back onto the ground, then found themselves back in the real world inside actual bodies. They weren't dead after all.

Kiera fell off the windowsill she'd been sitting on and landed on the carpet of Ezra's dorm. As she pulled herself up, pressing both hands to her jaw to ensure it was still intact, she saw Ezra leap out of his bed. He'd gotten his energy back and his eyes were dark.

"Whatever they needed," he told Kiera, helping her to her feet, "they got it and are ready to come back into the real world after a thousand years in exile."

As if on cue, both of them turned as they heard a loud crash and explosion, followed by screams of men and women outside. It was followed by shouting and the whoosh and whirs of spells being cast.

"The people out there don't realize that if they use spells on the gods, it will only give Vara and Kilon more magic," Ezra said as they rushed toward the bedroom door together. "I've seen enough of them to know we'll need to use natural means to bring them down."

"Are you talking about guns and swords?" Kiera asked as they rushed down the hallway toward the elevator. That felt very unlike Ezra, who used magic to solve most things.

"As far as I can tell. Though by the time we reach them, the gods might be too big and powerful to overcome with tanks, let alone swords."

"Then what can we do?"

Ezra paused and turned to her, fear and insecurity written on his face. "Fight, I guess. Better to fight and die together than to get torn apart."

They squeezed each other's hands, agreeing that they might die but glad they weren't doing it alone. She whispered the three words she'd wanted to say in his ear, making the tips of his ears turn pink, then they headed into the elevator, ready to face Kent one more time. If they died, at least Kiera could do it with few regrets.

27

"**W**hy do you think they drained us first?" Kiera asked Ezra as the elevator went down excruciatingly slow.

"Maybe they viewed us as the greatest threat and wanted us weak." Ezra shrugged, muttering spells under his breath as they descended. "It doesn't matter. We have to focus on killing them first. Why they did what they did can be worried about after."

But it felt important to Kiera. Vara mentioned saving her and Ezra for the future. Why would she do that when they'd been such a hassle up to this point? What else was she planning to do with them? What was her plan B if things went south?

The elevator doors opened and it was a quick

dash to the front door of the dorm building. They could hear more chaos outside but weren't sure what to expect as they rushed through the entrance. What they found was worse than Kiera had pictured.

The first thing they noticed were the two deities standing in the middle of the plaza, or rather crawling out from under it. Where the fountain used to be was now a hole, in which Vara and Kilon were roughly ascending. Their bodies, which had been seven to eight feet tall in the spirit world, were now massive, at least ten feet tall or more, and they looked otherworldly in their appearance. While Vara was beautiful and alluring, her hair and clothes interwoven with plants and stars, Kilon was horrifying. His sharp facial features coupled with the many weapons he bore on his front and back sent tremors through Kiera's body even though she'd already encountered him multiple times. At least in the spirit world, the two had been somewhat concealed by shadows and fuzzy memories. Here, they were larger than life.

The pair were climbing out of their tomb and allowing the magicians and teachers to shoot magical beams of light, flame, electricity, and acid at them. None of the elements did any damage. Instead, Kilon seemed to welcome the attacks.

Every time he was hit, he seemed to move faster. Just as Ezra said, the magic was strengthening him. Only physical attacks could actually harm him, and even then, Kiera wasn't sure what good a gun could do against a magic-infused god.

Students ran past Kiera and Ezra, fleeing the scene. Only a few were brave enough to help, and they probably wished they had run to as Kilon drew an axe from his assortment of weapons, the silver strings sewing his mouth shut reflecting the sun moments before he drove the blade down on a row of people. Screams overpowered the sound of Kilon's footsteps and even some of the magicians started to run away, using teleportation or speed spells to flee. One of those sorry men was picked up by Kilon before he could fully teleport and the magic disappeared into Kilon's hand instead, being absorbed before he crushed the man between his massive fingers.

"We have to do something!" Ezra shouted, then used magic to heave a bench at the giant god's head. Kiera noticed, thanks to her growing consciousness of magic, that he used a spell that wouldn't linger on the material being thrown. That way, the bench would only damage Kilon and not give him new magic as well. Kilon barely flinched when the bench hit him right in the eye. It did get his attention, though. After dropping the bloody mess that used to be a magician, he turned toward Ezra and Kiera, amusement flickering across his normally expressionless face.

"Be careful," Kiera warned as Ezra threw something else. "You don't have much magic to use. If you overwork it, it'll fizzle out completely like mine did."

"I'll bear that in mind," he said, then motioned for her to run. "Go. You can't use magic, so there's nothing you can do."

"I can warn you when to duck," Kiera countered. "We agreed to do this together, remember?"

"Of course I remember." He smirked, making jokes even now. "It was just a few minutes ago. Get behind me, then, and try to think of some other solution. You spent half a year studying without me. Try to remember some weakness this pair might have."

Kiera frowned, wracking her brain for anything useful. What she did know was that these two had been put away before by the gods, though it clearly hadn't been permanent. Sadly, there weren't any spells available to contact said gods and even if there were, Kiera didn't have the magic to do it anymore.

She cringed as someone flew past her, thrown

by Kilon or Vara. The gods were treating these people like toys, mimicking a cat messing around with a mouse. That or they weren't actually as powerful as they appeared. Now that she thought about it, they weren't using any magic. They were just using their physical forms to abuse.

"Got anything?" Ezra asked as he cast a few more spells. She saw his arms shaking as he held them up. He was weakening.

Before she could answer, Kiera saw the stone statue of Kilon from the tomb come flying toward them and they both had to duck out of the way. A second after that, Vara's statue came too. Kiera had to crawl across the ground to avoid it.

"I thought they didn't want to kill us," she muttered, watching Vara stomp on a female police officer. Then something behind them caught her eye. She could see Kent standing near Vara, his arms raised and eyes glowing red as he laughed maniacally. It looked like his brain had finally crumbled, becoming nothing more than a puppet for these two to use as they wished.

Wait. That might be the solution.

"Kent's the one who brought them magic and souls," Kiera shouted to Ezra as he leapt out of the way of a flying boulder. "They might be using him as a conduit for the magic, at least until they steal enough magic to not need him anymore." This battle was already strengthening them. If they managed to steal the souls of an entire army, which would inevitably come after them when news of this catastrophe spread, then Kent would be obsolete.

Ezra glared at his brother, then nodded. "We'll have to kill him. He may be powerful but he's no god."

Despite looking like a burnt remnant of a man, Kent could still bleed. He might be the only thing tethering these deities to this world. He was the string that had to be cut.

Kiera's senses confirmed it as they started to circle around Kilon, ducking through the trees to avoid the gods so they could get at Kent. As they went, Ezra grabbed a few stones and a stick that could serve as a sword. Even without a metal blade, a stick could still pierce a man's skin.

"Ezra!" They were halfway there when Kent's voice echoed toward them. "Do you think I'm blind?" His voice had the high pitch of insanity intermingled with his normal one. "We don't actually plan to kill you, so run and hide until it's all over." He sounded really resentful about the fact that he wasn't allowed to kill them.

Ezra opened his mouth but didn't speak. Kiera

could tell it tore him up to face off against his brother. It was Kiera's turn to do the talking.

"I thought you were desperate to kill me!" Kiera taunted, watching Kent through the trees. Vara was no longer with him. She and Kilon had gone ahead to grab the magic of the people escaping. "Or are you too scared to fight a couple of teenagers?"

Kent growled and she knew she'd injured his pride. Good. Now if only they had an actual plan to defeat him.

The two of them leapt into the open space again, landing on the paved path which was now cracking down the middle because of the hole the deities had created. Kent was waiting for them, but he was standing perfectly still. It made Kiera start to question whether Kent was being drained now too. Perhaps he'd been the one collecting the magic up until this point, and now the gods were taking it from him.

Sadly, that moment of peace didn't last. As Ezra raised his stick to hit Kent over the head and hopefully knock him out, Kent finally moved, ducking out of the way of the blow and punching Ezra right in the chest. It knocked him back and as Ezra stumbled, Kent yanked the stick out of his hands.

Tired of standing there uselessly, Kiera grabbed a stone and ran toward Kent to hit him with it. If none of them were using magic anyway, too afraid to lose it to their opponent, she might as well join in. She had no more magic to lose so there was little risk, other than him killing her, which now seemed unlikely because the goddess wanted her for some unknown reason.

Kent grabbed her arm and twisted it before she could land a blow. She used her other hand to punch him in the side, but other than making him wince, it didn't do much, and then she was shoved to the ground by the bottom of his boot before she could try any more pitiful attempts at combat. She was a necromancer, after all, not a soldier. Hand-to-hand combat wasn't her area of expertise.

As she lay on the ground, watching Ezra get back up and ready himself for another attack, she took a break to study the magic emanating from Kent. It was strong and, sure enough, it was connected to the two gods further down the path. She'd been right. He was feeding them.

Her heart swelled as she felt some of her own personal magic zipping in and out of Kent. It wasn't resisting his power over it, and that filled her with a strange protectiveness. He was using something that was hers and was treating it like a tool rather than a living, conscious thing like how she'd begun to view it.

If only I could bring it back. Kent only uses the magic for himself. I would use it to heal others.

As soon as the thought crossed her mind, she felt something in the magic shift. It moved slightly toward her. Just like when she asked her magic for help before and it had answered, perhaps it had been listening now, despite having to serve Kent. What made excitement leap into her chest was that it wasn't just her magic responding, though, it was other people's too. All the stolen magic was desperate to get away from Kent, she was realizing. It didn't want to be used for death. It wanted to be helpful to others.

"Ezra," she whispered to her boyfriend, who was standing next to her. His feet were angled forward on the ground, about to leap toward Kent. "I can stop him."

He must not have heard her, because he threw a rock at Kent, then jumped forward with his fists at the ready. He was trying to tackle Kent to the ground.

As the pair of brothers rolled around and beat each other, she decided it was better to just act before they ended up killing each other. Filling her thoughts with pleas and bargains to get the magic on her side, she leaned forward, reaching out her hands so they had a place to go.

Then she looked past Kent and Ezra and saw the gods turning toward her. Vara had a teenage boy screaming in her arms and as she made eye contact with Kiera, she tossed the boy over her shoulder like one would a pillow. The goddess's eye twitched and Kiera knew she'd been caught. The gods knew what she was up to. They might not want to kill her for convenience's sake, but that protection wouldn't last if she stole all the magic they'd spent years accumulating.

Kilon drew his gold-tipped bow from his back, notched an arrow, then aimed right at her. She had three seconds to get enough magic on her side and use it as a shield. Otherwise, that thing would cut right through her chest. It was as big as a spear.

No. Three seconds wasn't enough time.

She was dead.

28

As magic scampered away from Kent and toward Kiera, so did Kilon's arrow. It whizzed through the air, nearly sounding like an approaching missile and moving just as fast. She shut her eyes, attempting to duck out of its path but already knowing she wasn't fast enough.

Then a blue shield erupted around her, narrowly blocking the arrow before vanishing again.

Shocked, Kiera looked up to see who had done it.

"Stop sitting out in the open like that!" Ben shouted from the top of a nearby building before tossing a tree at Kilon. Meiying appeared beside him a moment later and added some pebbles to his attack, sending the small rocks forward at impossible speeds. Ben's tree hit Kilon in the face, preventing him from avoiding the stones, which cut through his arm and upper shoulder like shrapnel. The god didn't bleed, but his arm did fall to his side, useless for at least a moment.

A second later, Kiera spotted the other half of their team perched on a building across the path. Sally was the one who had cast the shield over Kiera and was currently doing it to her and Tucker as well. Meanwhile, Tucker was using magic to send the fleeing students and officers away faster so no more of them could die. Vara and Kilon's hands were already crimson from the blood of recent victims. They didn't need any more.

"Kill Kent or run!" Tucker shouted. "We'll hold the gods off... if that's even possible."

Luckily, the four teenagers weren't alone. Kiera could see a few other shimmers on the ground and neighboring buildings, meaning there were still some magicians remaining who were preparing an attack. The headmaster was probably among them. They weren't all dead yet and none of them planned to just surrender.

"Right." Kiera turned on Kent, who was on top of Ezra now and punching him in the face. It felt strange to see both of them using their hands instead of magic. Kent was probably unable to use his magic and power the gods at the same time, while Ezra had nothing left to use.

That left Kiera with the power. When that arrow had come toward her, she'd felt some of her magic return to her, accompanied by a bit more of every other victim's. She'd done it once. She could do it again.

Kiera grinned, unable to quell her excitement as more of the magic rushed into her. The hole inside her was filling again, then overflowing.

Kent punched Ezra in the cheek again, cutting him so Kiera could see white bone, and he grabbed a stone from the ground, preparing to drive it right into Ezra's eye. However, before he brought it down on his brother, Kent finally realized he was the one being drained and he turned toward Kiera with wide eyes. For a split second, his ruby irises flashed a normal brown again. He was losing his power.

"You!" His voice overflowed with complete and utter rage that this teen girlfriend of Ezra's had managed to undermine him with a mere thought. "You're dead! I don't care what Vara says! You're—"

Ezra suddenly grabbed a stone of his own and smashed the side of Kent's face with it. Blood spurt out of Kent's mouth and he finally fell onto his side. A small indent formed on the side of his head. Ezra sat up, coughing up blood of his own, and hit Kent again. Kiera crawled forward to stop him, worried he might start hitting Kent over and over like a madman, but he luckily stopped when Kent fell unconscious. Then Ezra dropped the bloody rock like it was poisoned. He turned toward Kiera, part of his cheek sagging from the massive gauge in it and his opposite eye was turning swollen and purple from all the punches he took.

"Whatever you're doing," he said, looking proud of her. "Keep it up."

Kiera didn't need to be told that twice. She got to her feet and kept bringing the magic to her, and eventually to Ezra when she sensed some of his magic heading toward her. Now that she could she could technically speak to the magic and have it actually listen, she was able to differentiate between different types and who they belonged to. The magic wasn't being controlled by her with brute force like what Kent had been doing. Instead, she was merely communicating with it and negotiating. The magic then chose to obey her of its own will.

Thirty feet away, the battle between the mages and the two gods raged on. The magicians who had been previously invisible were now working together with Ben, Tucker, Sally, and Meiying. They were hurling countless projectiles at the gods, shielding themselves, speeding about to avoid Kilon's arrows and Vara's fists, and using other forms of magic that couldn't feed the pair. Some summoned natural lightning from the sky or sent stones upwards before dropping them from incredible heights. Others created gargoyles like what Kent used against Kiera and sent them as suicide creatures to cut and gnaw at Kilon's ankles. One necromancer even teleported over a long dead mammoth and sent it barreling toward the gods, using it as a tusked puppet. Kiera might have enjoyed the spectacle if she wasn't so focused on draining all of Kent's remaining magic, then eventually taking what the gods had been using too. Stealing magic certainly didn't feel good. She felt like she'd just binged on a buffet and her stomach was now screaming from being overfilled, but this time it was her whole being an soul that was overwhelmed. Kiera wasn't a god. She wasn't built to have this much power. It had driven Kent insane and would do the same if she took any more without channeling the magic elsewhere.

Luckily, the headmaster appeared beside her a moment later and offered a solution.

29

"**S**orry I couldn't get here sooner," he told them both, panting as the battle continued in front of them. Kilon managed to grab a necromancer in the middle of casting a spell and squeezed him as he did the rest. He wasn't creative when it came to killing humans, though he was efficient.

"There's a spell," the headmaster continued, out of breath. "It's similar to what the former gods used to bring these two down before."

Kiera was about to ask how he knew about these gods and the old stories, but then remember that he and Kent used to be friends long ago so he must have learned all about it then. He used to be in the same shoes as she and Ezra were.

"But it's a spell that requires an insane amount

of magic," he continued. "Enough for a god to use. I don't—"

"Well, that's good," Kiera said quickly, feeling ready to collapse from all the magic she had in her now. "I have a whole lot of magic right now and nothing to do with it."

Headmaster Gillis chuckled nervously, then gestured for Ezra to come closer. "Hold hands. We'll channel the magic together while I recite the spell."

Ezra had been helping the others fight, since he now had most of his magic back, but he quickly obeyed his uncle as they formed a small circle. Kiera couldn't help glancing at Vara, waiting for her to turn and charge toward them to prevent them. The only thing that might prevent that was the goddess's own arrogant. It had gotten her banished before, though, so she might have learned from her mistakes, if the gods could even do that.

Headmaster Gillis cringed as he started reciting a spell. Unlike when Kent used dark necromancy spells in an evil, slithery language, this spell felt full of light and goodness. The language was smooth and jumped from one word to the next in a cheery manner, despite the headmaster's quivering voice. If it came from the God who banished Vara and Kilon, it must be a good God.

The magic finally poured out of Kiera, leaping into the path of the spell eagerly. Only her own original magic remained inside her, which made her feel the same way she had when she reunited with Ezra.

Kilon and Vara did finally turn toward the three of them as the spell began but by then it was to late. Kilon aimed his bow at the headmaster but Ben's spell placed a shield right in front of the arrow to block it.

Kiera gasped as long tendrils of light rose from the hole and wrapped around Vara and Kilon, dragging them back into the tomb where they'd been imprisoned hundreds of years ago. The goddess shrieked and thrashed about, her long arms knocking down the buildings around her and sending magicians and Kiera's friends alike flying through the air. But the headmaster didn't stop despite all this, determined to see through what he'd been fighting ever since he and Kent parted ways. The magic, combined with light from the very sun continued dragging the two protesting gods, or demons, down into the earth where they disappeared. Vara's screams died down, then ended completely, making way for silence.

The headmaster uttered the final words, then collapsed onto his knees, releasing Ezra and Kiera so he could sob into his own hands. His shoulders shook as he the tension eased from his shoulders. After feeling useless for so many years, filled with regrets about his past, he had finally saved as many as he could.

Ezra patted his uncle on the shoulder, then pulled Kiera into a hug. They clung to each other, unable to believe it was finally done. They could hear the magicians and healers calling out to each other, helping those who were injured or trapped under rubble. She heard Ben and Tucker's voices too. Although they'd fallen from the buildings, they'd survived. They probably used teleportation or feather fall to soften the blow. They were fine.

"We did it," Kiera said breathlessly, squeezing Ezra against her.

"Yeah." He sighed. "We did it."

They stood there a moment longer, an unconscious Kent and sobbing Phil at their feet, until Kiera felt the ground beneath her shift. She pulled back, making eye contact with Ezra again.

"Did you feel that—" she began, then felt herself tumbling backwards into the ground.

30

"I'm beginning to despite this place," Kiera told Ezra as they found themselves in the spirit realm once more. "Do you think Kent was pretending to be asleep?" He could have pulled them back here. The only other person who could was Vara.

"No. I used my magic to check." Ezra scanned their surroundings, keeping one hand on Kiera's when their bodies were more than little balls of light.

"Then that leaves only one person," Kiera whispered. "Vara, here to use her plan B." Vara must have kept them alive just in case they were banished again. This was her last resort. Kiera just couldn't figure out what exactly that plan was.

They both lingered in one spot, waiting for something to happen, but nothing did.

"Either she has plans," Ezra muttered, "Or she left us here to torture us as a final act of revenge. Neither of us know how to leave."

"You took me out once," Kiera said. "Can't you do that again?"

"My memories of the spell are fuzzy," Ezra answered. "He kept wiping our memories, remember? I don't want to risk getting it wrong and keeping us trapped forever."

"We're already trapped here forever."

"Well, the other option is killing the person who sent us here," Ezra added. "But we can't do that if we're alone."

"You know that one point about killing the sender but not the spell to get us out of here?" Kiera asked, both frustrated and trying to bring a joke into the tense situation. "Ezra—"

Finally, something popped into view. It was Vara and Kilon, but they didn't look tall and regal this time. They looked shriveled up, drained like how they'd made their victims looked. Their heights were more normal too, human. Vara was five-foot-four at the most and Kilon was six feet. These were their true forms. It made Kiera start to wonder if maybe they were just humans all along who got their hands on the wrong type of magic.

"You've been banished," Kiera told them, standing her ground and clasping Ezra's hand tightly. "Release us and die with dignity."

"Pretty words from a thief," Vara hissed, stepping toward her. Kilon did the same to Ezra.

Kiera tried to sense any magic around Vara and Kilon but there was none. They'd been completely emptied of all power. On the other hand, Kiera could feel hers and Ezra's magic present with them this time. It had followed them into this realm, once again proving Kiera didn't know everything about how this place worked. Having it by her side made her more confident. The magic was loyal to the good and noble, not to the selfish and cruel.

"Both of you are very powerful," Vara said, her voice just as seductive as normal. It had less effect when she looked so pathetic, though. "Your bodies are so full of life."

Kiera's eyes widened as Vara reached for her with both hands. She knew what they wanted.

"They're trying to steal our bodies!" Ezra shouted just as the pair of demons leapt toward them. Kiera could feel her soul resisting Vara's, fighting for control. There was a single moment when she feared Vara would win—after all, the goddess had lived for over a thousand years. She had more experience and spells at her fingertips.

However, as the magic swirled around Kiera and repelled Vara, she knew goodness would win out. The magic wanted nothing to do with these two evil beings.

Vara was knocked back, screeching like a cat as she fell to her knees, and a second later, Kiera saw Ezra shove Kilon away too. His magic was helping him, covering his body like armor. Ezra even flashed Kiera a genuine grin as he did so. They weren't afraid of these two wannabe gods anymore.

"It's time to embrace your deaths," Kiera said as Vara and Kilon's hands started to fade away. "Your judgement day has been delayed long enough."

Vara spat at Kiera as the last of her body disappeared, along with her husband's. Then, they were alone again and falling backwards, hopefully for the last time. Kiera didn't want to see this realm ever again. It should stay empty, just like it was before. The real world was harsh enough. No one needed a second realm at their fingertips.

"That was awesome—" Ezra started to say as they fell, then they both woke up in infirmary beds, grinning from ear to ear at their final victory. They weren't going to see those two gods again.

31

As soon as she returned to the land of the living, Kiera sat up and looked around. She was dressed in a white sheet rather than actual clothes and had to cover herself up quickly as she realized Ezra was in a bed right beside her. Hearing her, Ezra turned to her, still smiling. He then chuckled as he saw her reaction.

"You look beautiful," he assured her, which was probably a lie. His hair was all messy and his cheeks covered in bandages. She probably looked the same. He was still handsome but had definitely looked better.

They held eye contact for a moment, sharing their victory and love for each other in a single look, then Kiera heard the voice of her parents outside the curtains surrounding them and turned back to the front of the room.

The rest of the room had been hidden by some hospital curtains, but as soon as the people on the other side heard Kiera sit up and squeak from her sorry excuse for an outfit, the curtains were thrown back and her mother rushed in with her father right at her heels. Kiera was immediately enveloped in a huge group hug and by the time she had pushed her mother away to avoid suffocation, she could see Ezra's parents standing next to him, asking how he felt. He looked relieved to see them.

"I was so worried about you," Kiera's mom said.

"This magic business is far more dangerous than I initially thought," her father added. "It's bad enough having to worry about your mother but you too—"

Kiera tuned them out for a second to listen to Ezra's response.

"I'm sorry about Kent," he said quietly, looking down at the cracks on his knuckles. "I wish—"

"No, we should be the sorry ones," his mother interrupted, resting a hand on his shoulder. "You did the best you could. Char—Phil told us everything. We're beyond proud of what you did."

The hesitant smile on Ezra's face made the edges of Kiera's eyes sting. He had waited so long to be complimented by his strict parents and to live up to their expectations. Now he finally got to hear it, though it had only come after his brother nearly killed him.

"Where's Kent?" Kiera asked everyone, dreading any answer that wasn't about him being in a magical prison.

Ezra's mother turned toward her, her pretty face drooping down at the mention of her son. "He's been placed in prison and put on constant watch. We lied to ourselves when we gave him a second and third chance. That won't be happening again."

Ezra's father lowered his head, looking ashamed for their past leniencies and sorry that his son couldn't be redeemed. "We're sorry you and your family had to get involved," the tall father said, turning to Kiera's parents. "We'll try to compensate—"

"Oh, no. I've had my fair share of family drama," Kiera's mother cut in, waving the notion away with her hand. "It happens in every family, even magical ones. You don't owe us a thing. If anything, Kiera's caused your son just as much trouble... Well, not *just as much* but enough." She laughed at her own slip of the tongue. "What matters is that they're alive and well."

Kiera glanced at Ezra, wondering how relations

between their parents would go from now on. Kiera's parents knew she had a crush on Ezra and planned to date him, but she didn't know how much his parents were aware of it. That would make for a long, complicated conversation later. For now, probably best to keep a lid on it and save it for another day.

"Speaking of alive and well, your friends have been waiting outside your door for three hours," Kiera's dad said meekly. "I promised I'd call them as soon as you two were well—"

Before he could continue his sentence, Ben charged through the infirmary door, shouting Kiera's name and dragging Meiying in along with him. Tucker and Sally came in after, though their entrance was a little less chaotic. All four of them had bandages and Sally's arm was in a sling but other than that, they all looked fine and excited to discuss the fight.

"I'm a hero out there!" Ben said after giving both Kiera and Ezra a hug. "We thought the serial killer thing was a big deal but now we're all over the news stations in every part of the world. I've already done three interviews and bet I can bring an ad deal out of this situation!"

Meiying just shook her head at her boyfriend's

antics. Kiera was just glad he hadn't been trauma-tized by any of this.

The infirmary filled with the voices of her loved ones, as well as everyone's magic flitting about like butterflies and puppies. Kiera couldn't feel any happier than she did at this moment. As Ben continued narrating the battle to the parents, making Kiera's dad gasp at several points, Kiera reached over and held Ezra's hand.

They'd made it out alive and stronger than ever.

She wished this moment could last a lifetime.

❀ 32 ❀

The semester continued without any more mishaps. Headmaster Gillis got to keep his job, thanks to his instrumental spell that turned the tide of the battle, and Kiera graduated with moderately high grades, though it couldn't compare to Ezra's and Ben's. Once exams rolled around, Kiera started applying to magical medical schools and started discussing a long-distance relationship with Ezra. He wanted to go with her but since Dreadmore had always been his plan, they both decided one or two years apart wouldn't make a huge difference. If life or death situations couldn't tear them apart, a few hundred miles wouldn't. Plus, with magic, they could meet up as often as they wanted with little issue.

Ezra was leaning toward getting a teacher's

degree in magic. All his time helping out Kiera and training her had shown him just how much he enjoyed teaching others. Since Dreadmore had a pretty good teaching major available, he decided that was the best option. Then once he graduated, he could teach anywhere he wanted and Kiera could do the same with a medical degree. That meant marriage would be simple as could be. Not that marriage was immediately on the table, of course. They were just about to turn twenty. That still felt a little early. But she could tell both she and Ezra were looking forward to it when the time came. It might make for a nice graduation gift to each other.

The graduation ceremony was bittersweet. As Kiera walked across the stage to accept her diploma and saw all her friends in the seats, cheering her on, it fully hit her that she wouldn't be able to see them again every day like she used to. Their meals would be spent apart. It was painful to picture all of them having fun without her.

But then she locked eyes with Ezra as the diploma was handed to her and the look on his face, his eyes crinkled from a big smile and his teeth showing slightly, told her everything would be okay. Two years wasn't that long in the grand scheme of things. Plus, knowing Ben, he and Meiying would probably buy a house right next to Kiera and Ezra's.

She and Ben were lifelong neighbors and Ben had said so during their pre-graduation party.

Applause followed her down the steps with her Dreadmore Associate's degree, which would help her get into any academy she wanted from now on. She'd earned it.

Once the ceremony was over, complete with the roar of a rented dragon accompanying the closing music, she and Ezra walked hand and hand down the path one more time, headed toward the center of the plaza where the hole the Vara and Kilon had created was blocked off. The headmaster had promised to give them the honors of closing it, since they were the ones who fought them off. Plus, the headmaster apparently wanted it to serve as a reminder to everyone on staff that danger could be lurking right under your feet and one should always be vigilant.

The couple stopped in front of the gaping hole, looking down into the darkness where tendrils of light had dragged the evil pair. Ezra squeezed Kiera's hand.

"Shall we?" he asked, an open spell book in his other hand. He looked eager to use such a high-level spell and Kiera could tell her magic felt the same way. "Together?"

She squeezed his hand back. "Together."

They spoke the spell together, sending their magic daintily across the hole and sending the earth and stone back into the hole, filling it up and making the path even more beautiful than it was before. Kiera used her growth spell to spring up several pink and blue flowers along the path, They had taken something harmful and evil and created something beautiful that would last for generations.

When the path was covered and looked good as new, Ezra and Kiera walked away from it hand in hand, happy to leave it all behind and start a new adventure. Their friends met up with them halfway and they all left the campus to attend a second post-graduation party, enjoying their last bit of youth before adulthood hit.

Two years ago, Kiera came here alone and dreading the time she would spend in Dreadmore Academy. Now she was leaving it with a newfound family and companion magic that would remain loyal to her until death.

The old Kiera never would have believed her if she told her about it.

Click for more Mia Hall books!

Sign up for Mia's Newsletter to find out about releases.
Put the following in your browser window:
mailerlite.com/webforms/landing/e1d4k4